THE CODE

by Alexandra Powe Allred

SUMMIT BOOKS

Cover Illustration: Kay Salem

Dedication

For Ms. Patricia Caston
You are Grandma, Mama, and Ms. Whitley—
A great friend, teacher, and motherly soul

About the Author

Alexandra Powe Allred has a B.A. from Texas A & M University, where she majored in history and minored in Russian. As the daughter of a U.S. diplomat, Allred spent many years overseas, in Russia, Tunisia, Iraq, and Germany.

In 1994, she was named Athlete of the Year by the U.S. Olympic Committee and won a gold medal at the U.S. Nationals in women's bobsledding.

She is the author of several sports books including *Entering the Mother Zone* and *The Quiet Storm.* In addition, she has written *Passion Rules! Inspiring Women in Business* and a dog obedience book.

Currently, Allred maintains her passion for sports as a professional football player for the WPFL's Austin Rage. She is raising three young children with her husband, Robb.

For information, contact
Perfection Learning® Corporation
1000 North Second Avenue, P.O. Box 500
Logan, Iowa 51546-0500.
Phone: 800-831-4190 • Fax: 712-644-2392
perfectionlearning.com

PB ISBN-13: 978-0-7891-5692-1
PB ISBN-10: 0-7891-5692-x
RLB ISBN-13: 978-0-7569-0693-1
RLB ISBN-10: 0-7569-0693-8
Printed in the U.S.A.
7 8 9 10 PP 19 18 17 16

ONE

HE was running for his life. His legs were pounding the ground so hard he could feel the vibrations. His arms were pumping, but the guys were still behind him. He could hear them. He could feel them.

Everything looked strange to him. He tried very hard to remember just where he was. He was trying to get back to his neighborhood, but every time he turned a corner, he seemed to go farther and farther from his block.

He was pumping it. He was running with everything he had. As he turned up another street, he glanced behind him. There were four of them. They were catching up fast.

The one in front was the one who had first yelled at him. That one was wearing a blue bandanna around his head, kind of low down just over his eyebrows. He had an earring—the whole bit. He was one of those guys you're supposed to stay far away from. He was tough.

The next one behind him had on a blue

bandanna too, but over it he had a baseball cap. He wore the cap backwards. He was smiling. He knew that the kid was scared to death, and he thought it was funny. While he ran, he joked loudly about what he was going to do to the kid when he caught him. The two behind him wore almost the same things—blue bandanna or cap, jeans, and some sort of blue shirt that looked the same. It was "their" color.

That's how the whole thing had started. The kid was wearing a blue sweat suit. That made them mad because the color blue is one of their gang's markers—it's theirs. You've got to respect what's theirs—their property, their territory, even the colors they claim as theirs. If they catch you wearing colors that belong to their gang, you're stupid. You're history.

The only thing worse than wearing their colors is wearing the colors of another gang. Then they think you're the enemy, and you're really history. But that's the code of the street. If you don't know the code, don't go on the streets.

He looked back and kept running hard. He ran right through a game of kickball. That's when I first saw him. Man, he was flying. His face was washed with sweat. I guessed that he had been running for a while. He was wearing blue sweatpants with a blue sweat jacket that zipped up the front. He wore high tops. They looked new. Expensive. Then, I saw why he was running. It was the Jags. Four of them anyway. They were riled. Ripper was out in front. He was yelling and carrying on. He wanted that boy bad. The ground shook when they passed by. They were hitting the pavement hard. And they were gaining.

❖ ❖ ❖

The bell rang, and I jumped. I didn't realize how far into my story I was. Remembering that kid and that day really took me back, I guess. I looked at Ms. Whitley. She turned and looked at me. I kind of smiled. I don't know how she always knows when I look at her, but she does. She smiled back and motioned for me to come over. I pulled my stuff together and slid out of my desk.

I like Ms. Whitley. When I was little, there was this thing, you know, that you could never let anyone know that you liked your teacher, but I'm past that now. She's real cool. She laughs and jokes with kids, and she's easy to talk to.

I set my book and journal down on her desk and looked around. Old habit, I guess. You still don't want *too* many people to see you talking to the teacher after class. It was safe, though. The class was empty. I could hear kids hollering and banging lockers out in the hallway.

"What's up?" She lets me talk to her that way.

"Just wondering what you were writing." She looked down at my journal. "You were pretty intense there for a while. Can I see it?" She smiled and spread out her hands.

"I thought you said it was due next week." I wasn't ready for her to see it yet. I didn't even know if I was going to turn it in. It felt really weird writing about it, reliving it.

"I know," she said as she turned her head to the side, "but you know how much I love your stories. I'll bet this one is going to be good. What's it about?" She was like a little kid getting all excited about a present. She acts like schoolwork is the greatest thing in the world. I swear, when someone gets an A, especially a kid who usually doesn't, she is more excited than he is. *You see what you can do,* she says. *See how well you can do when you try!*

"Just about this kid who came into our neighborhood once," I shrugged. "This stupid kid."

She raised her eyebrows at me. She didn't understand. Why would I want to write about a stupid kid? Why couldn't I get that kid out of my head? I'd seen bad stuff go down before, you know? So I couldn't understand why he'd stuck in my head. Maybe because he was the beginning of the end . . .

She made a face at me. She mashes her face all up so she looks sort of crazy, but she only does that with the kids she really likes. It always makes me feel good. Sometimes I'll be thinking hard or something and look at her, and she'll make that face. I know that she's been watching me and is happy I'm trying so hard. I never make a face back. And I didn't this time. I just smiled like always, shrugged my shoulders like it was my secret, and picked up my story.

"Okay. See ya tomorrow, kiddo."

I kind of waved "bye" at her and went to my locker to get my jacket. While I was digging around in my locker, my buddy Taylor came over. Taylor Johnson is from my block, and we go to the same school. Taylor and I got put into a program that buses kids to another school, one of those magnet schools. That's what the education people call them. They've got these programs where certain schools focus on certain subjects, like math and science.

I got sent to a school that focuses on English and social sciences. Kids are allowed to pick what they're interested in, but no one ever asked me. I was "evaluated" and sent to Harriet E. Wilson. Harriet E. Wilson was the first African American (man or woman) to publish a book, and Mama said that was a good reason for me to go to Harriet E. Wilson. She said maybe I would be a famous writer one day. I know she said that because I write all the time. It's the one thing I can do that I like to do, and it's free. I do it because it helps me with things, but I guess some teachers thought it meant I was going to be a writer, so they sent me to Harriet E. Wilson.

We live in the District—Washington, D.C.—just off U Street, but Harriet E. Wilson is in Arlington, Virginia. It's over the Potomac River, 20 minutes from my house, but it's like a different world. We were taken out of the hood so that we could have a better chance for "interracial relations and education." Whatever.

Some people are afraid of where I live. I mean, I get worried about things. I'm not stupid. But it's home, you know? It's where my friends and my family are, where I grew up. I fit in just right. Arlington, Virginia, is all green hills, big houses, neatly trimmed hedges, and little sidewalks that wind up to each house. It's all spaced out; there's not a whole lot of traffic compared to home and plenty of places to play kickball. It's nice, but it's not home.

The first time I ever heard "nigger" wasn't at Harriet E. Wilson, but it was the first time I'd had it yelled straight to my face like I was the scum of the earth. It was really hard, you know? I mean, it's one thing to have your buddy yell it, being a jerk. That's bad enough. But this was different. It was like some kids hated my guts just because I was there. Now, five months later, I know who to stay away from. Most of the kids at school are cool. They don't seem to care that I'm black, and I don't really care that they're white or whatever they are. Like my grandma always says, "People is people."

Anyway, there Taylor was, jumping around my locker, acting all excited because school was out. I never did quite figure out how he got sent to Harriet E. Wilson. I wasn't complaining. I liked having him around.

"Say, man, what're you doing for your project?" Taylor had the same assignment as me from Ms. Whitley.

"I don't know yet."

"Yeah, then what were you so busy writing in there?"

He poked his finger at my journal.

"I was just, you know, doodlin' and stuff. I don't know what to write about yet."

Our assignment was to write about where we come from. We were supposed to pick a story that would represent our neighborhood, our background, or our home. As soon as Ms. Whitley passed out the assignment, I thought about that stupid kid again. Imagine dressing like that, looking the way he did, and coming into our neighborhood.

"Ms. Whitley doesn't know what she's askin'. She isn't from our block." Taylor shook his head. He hated this school. He hated being called names and feeling different.

I looked down the hall into Ms. Whitley's room. She was leaning over some papers. Her elbows were up on the desk, and her hands were clasped around her face. She's a hard thinker too. Little pieces of hair kept falling forward as she would try to tuck them behind her ears. She has real pretty hair. It goes to the middle of her back, so some days she wears it up in a bun, and other days she lets it hang down. I like it best when she wears it up. Her eyes are a dark brown, and her face is round and pretty. When she wears her hair up, she looks like a doll or something. A lot of the boys in the school have a crush on her. Not me. I just like her, you know?

But it was true what Taylor said. What could she know about U Street? You could tell by looking at her that she was probably rich or close to it growing up. She probably had her father pay for college, had a car when she turned 16, the whole thing. She wasn't spoiled—she's too cool for that. But she would never come to U Street. And if she ever did, like if she was lost or something, she would lock her car doors.

"What am I supposed to write about that she could understand? You wanna bet she was born in an all-white neighborhood and never had a brother in her school?" Taylor jabbed me with an elbow.

"Naw, she's not that way," I defended, and it was true. She doesn't care if a guy is poor or black or white. She likes everyone the same. People is people.

"So what are you going to write about?"

"I don't know yet." I shut my locker and walked down the hall with Taylor. When we got to the door, Taylor grabbed my journal out of my hands and took off running. I yelled at him and tried to catch him. We burst through the front doors of the school and out into the parking lot. He was dancing all around me and making stupid faces. He ran around the other side of some teachers' cars and stopped, grinning away. He opened up the journal, and his smile kind of faded. After a minute he looked up at me. His hands fell down to his sides.

"What's this?" he demanded. "What the hell are you writing about this for? You crazy?" He threw the journal at me. "Man!" And he turned and started to walk away.

"Hey," I yelled after him. I felt embarrassed, like I had betrayed him. "Hey, it's nothing. I was just writin' about it 'cause it was on my mind, you know? You sayin' you haven't thought about it? Hey, I'm not handin' that in. I was just writing." But Taylor kept walking.

I just stood there for a while. What could I say? It was true; I mean, I probably wasn't going to hand it in. Grandma told me that writing out your feelings helps sort through things. So I was sorting. Big deal.

I watched as Taylor got farther and farther away and remembered that day the kid came around. I remembered Ripper and how it all went down. Then I ran after Taylor.

TWO

I had been eating with Grandma when the story came on the news. It had been three weeks since it happened, but the story was still on.

Ripper and them had said that it would all blow over, but there it was. Grandma stopped eating and began shaking her head.

Grandma and I have been together all of my life. In some ways, she's more like my mom than my grandmother. Ma has always had to work long hours, so Grandma has always taken care of me. My dad took off when I was two. We haven't seen him since. I don't care if we ever do. We get along just fine without him.

Grandma moved in to help Ma with me. Then we applied for government housing. That was way before I can remember, though. It's something I sure don't talk about at school. I just say we've got an apartment. As it is, most kids at my school don't know what it's like to live in an apartment. But to tell them it's government housing? No way. They would think my mama's a bum or something because we stay there. They don't know she works two jobs, a day job and a night job. They don't know that my dad was a bum, that he left her all alone. I never used to see her because she was working all the time, but that's how it was. She was trying to take care of Grandma and me, and she didn't get paid too much. So we took extra help.

Grandma was clucking her tongue at the TV. "That poor boy. His poor family. How will they ever . . . ?" She spoke softly and shook her head. The television continued to talk to us.

"Police are still investigating the disappearance . . ."

I pushed away from the table. I felt sick. I didn't want to hear any more. I didn't want to hear how his mother and father were suffering. I didn't want to see pictures of his grandmother crying. I couldn't. I excused myself and went to my room. I fell down on my bed and tried to close my eyes. I squeezed them shut and threw the pillow over my face, but it didn't help. I could still see that kid's face. I thrashed around on my bed, but it was no use. I would never be able to clear my head. I sat up and saw my journal. I decided to write some more. Maybe it would help.

❉ ❉ ❉

They were close behind him. They had been too close when he tried to double back. I guess he realized he was only getting in deeper, so he would have to try to get back out again. He got about three feet ahead of the Jags, slipped behind a junk car, and started back toward us.

I could see his face real clear then. His eyes were wide, and his mouth was pulled tight. He was concentrating hard. He was focusing on the end of the street and pumping it hard.

Ripper had been close behind him, but Gilly was far enough behind them that when he saw the kid doubling back, he cut to the right and ran straight at him. The kid faked left, then right, then left again. Gilly fell to the right, and the kid squeezed past him. Gilly fell into Ripper's way, and they both stumbled.

The kid broke loose and was really running. He ripped it wide open. It wasn't until then that I realized Taylor had been yelling the whole time. I had been so busy watching the kid and the chase that I hadn't realized it was him. When the kid was close to us, Taylor came down the stairs we had been standing on. He whooped again. He had been yelling, "Get 'im, Ripper."

He got to the edge of the stairs and kicked the kid as he passed by.

The force knocked the kid to the side. He tried to put a hand out to catch himself, but he had been running too fast. He wiped out on his right side in the street. He hit hard too. He never had a chance to raise his head before the guys were on him. Ripper planted his knee in the middle of the kid's chest. The kid let out a grunt. It was the first sound I heard him make. Gilly, Brad, and Jackson were on him next. I couldn't even see the kid anymore. I just saw all the Jags kicking and punching. Then I heard the kid yell.

"Aieee!" He was screaming. He said something else in Spanish, but none of us could understand him.

"Speak English, boy! You in America!" someone yelled.

"Get 'im, Ripper!" Taylor was jumping up and down. "Get the Messkin." I looked at Taylor for a second when I heard him say that. It was the way he'd said it. I looked back at the kid. Was he Latino? I tried to see his face, but he had rolled over to one side and was trying to cover his head. They were beating him up bad. I could see some blood on Ripper.

In the afternoons my grandma watches her "stories"—soap operas—and I always make fun of them because when they break for a commercial, all the actors freeze and act like they're speechless. I tease her about that. So a lot of times I'll start to tell her we're out of milk or something and freeze, acting like her stories. She always throws something at me and laughs. Now all of a sudden, standing out there on the stoop, I couldn't say a word. I was like one of those dumb-looking actors—just staring.

I saw Jackson pull off the kid's shoes and Gilly rip off his jacket. I just stood there while Taylor cheered. I remember the Jones sisters standing down the street staring too. We were all stuck in the same awful story. And the kid couldn't do anything. He was getting kicked and punched, lying in a ball, just getting his clothes ripped off.

THREE

HIS name was Alberto Salvazar. He was from Peru. He and his family had just come from Peru to the United States and were staying with his father's family. His uncle had a pretty good job here and had talked his brother into coming to the United States. His uncle must have been pretty happy they were coming because when they got here, he had a big party for them. Alberto and his sister got gifts. Alberto got the sweat suit. He had decided to go for a walk or run in his new suit and look at the neighborhoods. Stupid kid. He had not been here long enough to have the rules explained to him. I guess that's how he wound up on our block. He probably wanted everyone to see his great new American clothes. He was probably hoping people would think he was from the United States. He probably just wanted to fit in.

I saw his mother and father on the news. They were speaking Spanish, but his uncle spoke English. He was saying he couldn't believe it, that they came here because they had a dream, and now it was ruined.

I have dreams now too. They're nightmares, though. But I used to have another dream. I used to dream that I could bring home money that would help Ma. I would make money, and then Ma could quit one of her jobs. She'd be like a regular mom. Grandma and I would eat dinner with her at 6:00, and Ma would be around to watch shows with Grandma. And Ripper had told me I could. He told us all that.

Ripper was the leader of the Jags. He had joined when he was 12 years old. He quit school and began working for his gang. They paid him good money to run errands and stuff for the big guys, and he took good care of his mama. He bought her new things, and nobody ever messed with her 'cause she was his mama.

I had been worrying about that a lot. Ma worked two jobs. I would hear all the time about people who would get robbed on their paydays. I was scared that one day she would be robbed. But if I belonged to the Jags, if I did stuff for Ripper, the word would be out, and no one around here would mess with her. And she wouldn't have to be out so late. She would be safer if I could help.

Ripper was 17 years old when he began running the Jags, and he was respected. Even the adults knew to leave him alone. He was the kind of guy you hear stories about and wonder if they're true, but no way would you ever ask. If Ripper ever heard you were asking questions about him, he would get real mad.

So that's how it had started. I had already begun really thinking about it—about joining the Jags and working for Ripper—when Taylor told me he was going to join. When I heard all that good stuff from Ripper about what I could do, it kind of changed my mind about what I had heard before about gangs.

Ma and other people were always saying that they needed to get rid of Ripper. They had thought when J. D. left, things would be okay again. But the Jags voted Ripper in as new leader, and everything started all over again. Only Ripper was even badder than J. D. He never allowed new people into the block without checking them out. He knew everything about everything. I had even seen him talking back to some cops. He wasn't afraid of nothing.

That's how it is in D.C. At least, in certain parts, like my neighborhood. Up by Pennsylvania Avenue, everything is real white, if you catch the meaning. All the politicians, all those senators and stuff, are broken up into different groups, some Democrats and some Republicans. And all day, every day, they argue over different things like welfare, abortion, or kids and drugs. Day after day. The government is a lot like Grandma's soaps. It's okay if you miss the news one day because it will be about the same story three days later.

My neighborhood is about 20 blocks up from Pennsylvania Avenue. Only things look a lot different. There are no huge, dome-shaped buildings with the American flag flying overhead. There are no cherry blossoms, no reflecting pond, no tourists, no neat sidewalks. There are four-story apartment rows, one after the other. To a stranger, I guess, they all look the same, but we can recognize and identify different homes by window dressings.

Emma Saunders has lacy curtains. They're about the nicest curtains up. Two stories up are red curtains. Really, they're sheets. That's my room. Our other window has a lacy curtain too, but it's not as nice as Ms. Saunders'. Across the hall from us is Old Man Lovelace. From the street you can see his mini blinds with a big chunk taken out of the right bottom half. He did that so his crazy cat could look out the window. He used to open the window, but one day his cat jumped out and broke her leg. So he keeps the window shut now. It'll be 100 degrees outside, but he won't open that window.

Below him lives the Powell family. They've got so many kids in that apartment, I don't know how they can live like that. I don't think they're supposed to have that many, but that's how it is. You live where you can, you know? So they never have their windows open 'cause someone is always sleeping in there. They've just got a heavy wool blanket nailed to the window. That's my apartment building.

But some things aren't so different from Pennsylvania Avenue. We've got different groups that are always fighting too, just like the Democrats and the Rebublicans. The Jags run most of my neighborhood, but over on 15th Street is the T-Posse gang.

I can't really remember when the T-Posse and the Jags first got into it, but they were in a full-out war. It wasn't like two kids fighting after school, either. It was bad. While I know the politicians don't actually kill one another, they fight just like the Jags and the T-Posse—over power. It's all about who is the strongest, who has the most territory, and who scares people the most.

You know, the president wants all the politicians to be afraid of him, not to challenge him on laws he wants to pass, but they do. That's how it was with Ripper. He had a reputation. Gangs from other neighborhoods knew about him and were afraid of him, but they still tried to challenge him. They would try to see if they could get away with things, like stepping into his territory, selling drugs in our neighborhoods, ripping him off. It was all about power. It was the code of the street.

So now I'd better start from the beginning—from when I started running with the Jags.

FOUR

ONE day I was sitting on the stoop, just hanging out, when Ripper and Gilly came up to me. Ripper told me that he had been watching me and liked what he saw. He said he knew I was smart and faithful. He was going to bet that he could trust me and that I would never turn on a brother.

At first, I wasn't too sure about talking to him. He was kind of scary. But then he talked to me about school. I figured for sure he would say "get out" or that school was a waste of time, but he said that I should stay in and that it was cool that I got good grades. He said that there aren't enough African American leaders in this country, and the only way to change that is to keep the young brothers in school. Later, he would say stuff that didn't ring right, but he said the right things then, like a politician, you know? He suckered me good. When I told my mother about that, she said Ripper was absolutely right. She said she was surprised but glad to hear that

Ripper thought that way. Still, she did not want me talking to him.

"He's got the right ideas, but he's twisted them all around," she said and shook her head at Grandma. "He's got some nerve wearing that hat. You seen that hat he's wearing?"

"Yes, I've seen it," Grandma said. They were talking about his Malcolm X hat. It was all black and had a big white X on the front. I had been wanting one too. Everyone was wearing one.

"I'll bet you he doesn't even know what the *X* stands for, let alone what Malcolm X really wanted." Ma kind of snorted with disgust. Suddenly I realized that I didn't know what the *X* stood for either. I was thinking about asking when she looked up at me and asked if I knew. I tried to play it off like I knew and, oh, wasn't Ripper stupid for not knowing, but she saw through that.

"Here," she said and pulled one of the kitchen chairs out for me to sit down. "Do you know what his real last name was?"

I shrugged.

"You see there, it's bad enough that the kids don't learn it in school, but they don't even bother to learn it when the man becomes popular again." Ma shook her head at Grandma and sat down on the other side of me.

"Steven, when you see Malcolm X on TV, you know what you're seeing?" She leaned in real close to me and studied my face. When she did this, I listened very hard. "You're only seeing part of who Malcolm X was. You're seeing the angry part. He preached that the white man was the devil, and the black man must get power and respect by any means possible!" She waved her hands in the air like she was imitating Malcolm X. I had seen tapes of him preaching to great big groups of blacks and yelling that we had to take control of our lives, our neighborhoods, and our schools. Things like that. It sounded good to me. Man, imagine being at school, wherever I wanted to be, and not having to look over my shoulder, always wondering if someone was talking about me like I don't belong. Malcolm X said things like we had to learn to take care of ourselves and not rely on the government for handouts. I remembered the things he'd said, and I nodded at Ma. She was still talking.

"He scared a lot of people. A lot of white folks," and she kind of chuckled. "Can't say that I blame them. It's scary to hear those things. I know 'cause I grew up hearing them from white people."

"What things?" I asked.

"Malcolm hated whites as much as some whites hated blacks, and he wasn't shy about telling people. That scared a lot of folks." Grandma was nodding as Ma spoke.

"It was one thing to have a white hating a black. People could accept that," Grandma laughed sarcastically. "Oh, but have a black man talking about such things and whoa!" She threw her hands up.

"This was right around the time when Dr. Martin Luther King was working with the civil rights movement," Ma said. "They were trying to spread the word about nonviolent demonstration. Malcolm X and Martin Luther King were on complete opposite ends of how to win rights for black folks."

"In the beginning," Grandma interrupted.

"That's right!" Ma said. "But as Malcolm got older, he realized that Martin Luther King wasn't so far off. You see, Malcolm X had been treated terribly by whites all his life, and he honestly believed that blacks and whites just couldn't live together." Ma shrugged her shoulders and looked kind of sad when she said this.

"But when he traveled to Mecca, he saw how beautifully all the blacks and whites got along. It changed his way of thinking. By the time he came back to the United States, he understood that the problem here was with the system, not with blacks and whites. But when he started to break ties with the Nation . . ."

"Why did he go to Mecca?" I asked. I wanted to ask about the Nation too, but was afraid for them to see how little I knew about Malcolm X. There were a lot of Muslims in my neighborhood. More and more lately, but I didn't really know what they believed. When I asked Ma, she took a deep breath, and I could tell that it was going to be one of those answers that was long and complicated. She was thinking about how to answer me when Grandma cut in.

"Isn't this black history month?" she asked, but it wasn't really a question. She knew the answer. "Why aren't you talking about this in class?"

"What are you talking about right now?" Ma asked. "In social studies, I mean."

"Well," I shrugged my shoulders, "the Constitution." It was true that we were discussing the civil rights movement a little bit but nothing about Malcolm X.

"I'll tell you what I want you to do. I want you to ask about it tomorrow. Ask your teacher if you can discuss Malcolm X and how he fits into everything. It'll be good for the other kids too."

Ma looked up at Grandma and nodded her head. And that was that. Whenever they both decided something should be a certain way, there was no more talking about it. I knew if I didn't say something about it in class, Ma would probably call the school and ask. What she didn't understand was there were hardly any black kids in the whole school. If I raised my hand to ask about Malcolm X, all the other kids would say it was just because I'm black and he was black. I figured the teacher would blow me off too.

But I was surprised. It was third period, and I was in Mr. Peterson's class. He is my social studies teacher. He's also the football coach. He is tall and big. Not fat, but real thick. From my seat he doesn't seem so big, but whenever I have to go up and ask a question, he seems huge. Everyone looks tiny compared to him, even the other teachers. He has bright red hair and a full beard and mustache that are just as bright. All the kids call him Paul Bunyan.

When the bell rang and the class was seated, I raised my hand. I figured I would ask and get it over with. Mr. Peterson lifted his chin toward the ceiling and stared down at me. That's his way of recognizing someone to talk. His hands are always shoved into his pockets.

"Um, I was wondering if we could talk about Malcolm X at all." I could feel everyone looking at me, and I shifted in my seat a little. "I mean, like what was his real last name, and what does the *X* stand for and . . ."

"That is an excellent idea," Mr. Peterson said. He turned toward the chalkboard and grabbed a piece of chalk. The other hand was still in his pocket, but he swung the one holding the chalk around at the class. "I'll bet that less than half the class—no, I'll bet that only a few of you can answer those questions. Let's see, what were they? What is the *X* for? What is his . . ." He turned back toward the board and began muttering to himself as he wrote. He wrote down the questions I had asked, plus a few more. When he was finished, he turned back to the class.

"Well?" he shrugged his shoulders. No one said a word. "No one?" He was still waiting, but no one raised a hand. "Unbelievable!" He shook his head. "Well, Steve, it looks like you've stumbled onto something here. We all know about Martin Luther King, but . . . don't we?" He looked around the class, and everyone nodded. "Well, thank goodness for that, at least," he mumbled, "but I tell you, Malcolm Little was a very interesting fellow. Well, suppose you tell me what you do know about Malcolm X."

For the rest of the period, people said what they had heard about him. Big surprise, it wasn't good. They called him things like a racist, evil, a big mouth, and dangerous. Tammy Henderson said that her mother said that Malcolm X was no better than the Ku Klux Klan. Mr. Peterson mostly listened to what everyone said. At the end of class, he gave us our new assignment. We were to find out as much as we could about Malcolm X by the next class, and he said he would do a little research and find a good book for us to read since there wasn't much about him in the books the school gave us.

FIVE

Taylor jumped in to the Jags first. He didn't have to tell me. I knew. He was beaten up. Not too bad. Enough to show he'd been jumped, but not as bad as you'd think. Getting jumped was the way of getting into the gang. They probably went light on him because of Brad. Ripper had told Taylor the same stuff he told me about the Jags, only Taylor didn't have anyone at home to tell him not to join. He only had his brother, and Brad was already a member of the Jags. Brad got jumped about two years ago and had nothing but good things to say about the gang. He made money and friends. He had told Taylor that he'd let him join when Taylor was 13.

Taylor worshiped his brother. Maybe I just don't understand because I never had a brother, but I always thought Brad was kind of a jerk. He ran around and acted like some big shot because he was with Ripper, but he always did whatever Ripper told him to do. He was like a puppy, you know? I always thought that if I belonged to a gang, I would be a leader, not a guy who takes orders. But that's how Taylor got in—he went to a meeting and got jumped in. He said that he was sworn to secrecy and could not betray the code of the Jags. He told me that he could only talk to me about that stuff if I joined. But that's not why I joined. Okay, it helped, but when I saw that Taylor was making money . . .

It was about a week after he joined when I noticed the change. He was a lot more serious. He was acting different, even around me. It was like he was grown-up all of a sudden. He was talking about important things he had to do, that he had to "tend to business" and things like that. I kept asking him what, but he kept saying that he couldn't betray his brothers. What's that about? After all the stuff we'd been through together, he was suddenly choosing those guys over me. That made me mad.

One day after school, I followed him. He went to Ripper's, then to the store on the corner of 14th and W Streets. We went there sometimes in the summer to get sodas and snow cones when it was really hot. My ma said that an ice cream man used to come into our neighborhood, but not anymore. Shoot, we can barely get the cops to come in. It's like I said, if strangers come into our neighborhood, most times you can bet they're lost. Cops included. Anyway, Taylor went into the store, and about a minute later, he walked out with a paper bag. I came around the corner and stood in front of him.

"Whacha doing?" I stared at his bag. He shifted it into another hand.

"You followin' me?" He squinted at me.

"What's in the bag?" He had been acting so cool, and now I was going to find out what it was about.

"Look," he said real seriously. He looked over his shoulder and pushed me around the corner. "If I show you, you swear not to tell?" I nodded.

He opened the bag and I peered into it. In it was a gun. A handgun. Taylor closed the bag again. I couldn't believe it. I thought that Taylor knew better than that. Guns are bad news. I guess he knew what I was thinking because he shrugged his shoulders and started to walk again. I followed.

"Hey, it's not like it's for me. But when I deliver this, I'm gonna get $50. Can you believe that? Just for pickin' up a bag."

"Yeah, who's gonna give you that?" But I knew. I knew that Taylor wasn't making up stories. That was how Ripper operated; I had heard stories about him.

"Ripper has me pick up deliveries, and he pays me when I bring 'em to him." He smiled. He was pretty proud of his new job.

"You fool," I practically laughed. "You know what would happen if you were caught with the bag? And do you really think Ripper would admit the gun was his?" I laughed right at him this time. "No way, man. He'd say he didn't even know you."

"Naw, he's cool. He takes care of his own. Besides, who would ever suspect a kid?"

That wasn't Taylor talking; that was Ripper again.

We walked for a while without saying anything. It was hard to believe that Taylor was delivering a gun and didn't think anything about it. It was hard to believe that he was getting paid $50 for taking a bag to someone.

We turned up our street, and I could see Ripper and Gilly sitting on the stoop in front of Gilly's building. Gilly's building was two down from mine. There were a few cars parked outside. There was an old 1980 red Camaro with all the windows busted out. No one owned it. It had just appeared one night. Some of the neighborhood guys lifted it, went joyriding, and dumped it. It was kind of a joke, you know? You could steal a car, ride around in it, and dump it on your own turf 'cause no cops were coming into our neighborhood. Whoever the sucker was who owned this car was never going to see it again, and it was in plain sight.

Ripper and Gilly were using the car as target practice, chucking rocks and pieces of cement from the crumbling entrance stairs to Gilly's building. They stopped talking when they saw us coming. They didn't smile or wave or anything. They just sat there and stared at us while we walked up the street. I peeked at Taylor out of the corner of my eye. I could feel how stiff he was. He had broken the code of silence by letting me walk with him, and he was scared. We didn't say a word to each other until we were right next to them. Ripper threw the piece of cement in his hand, taking out the whole rear window.

"What's up, boy?" Ripper was looking straight at me. He was working on a slow smile. "You decide to join the team?" It was a full smile now.

"I, uh, don't know. I was just walkin' with him." I kind of shuffled my feet a little.

"You talkin' about business to my man here?" he said to Taylor.

"Huh?" Taylor jerked his head up. "No way, Ripper. He knows the score, but I asked him to think about jumpin' in." He kind of smiled so that Ripper would think everything was cool.

"Good man. You know what to do with the bag?" He kind of jerked his head, and Taylor jumped to attention.

"Yeah." Taylor ran up the stairs to the building and disappeared through the dark doorway. Gilly stood slowly and looked around real cool for a minute. Then he followed Taylor inside. I stood alone with Ripper. While I stared at the doorway, I could feel his stare on me. I turned back to him.

"So, how's your mama?" he asked.

I just stared at him. I kicked at some of the rubble on the stairs. These stairs were just like mine. It's not like we can call our landlord. We don't have one, not really. So things fall apart. Front steps crumble away, broken toilets go without fixing, and stoves rattle.

"I hear she works two jobs. That's rough, man. It ain't right that a guy can never see his mama 'cause she's always workin'." He shook his head like he really felt sorry for me.

"Yeah," I agreed. What else could I say? He was right, and we both knew it. I picked up a pebble and tossed it at the car. It bounced off the door and bounced on the pavement. This amused Ripper, and he kind of chuckled in his fist.

Taylor appeared at the doorway. He looked at Ripper and hesitated a little. Then he came down toward me and smiled.

"Let's go." He turned to Ripper. "Tonight?"

Ripper nodded, and Taylor motioned for me to follow him. Ripper just stared at me.

"See ya, Ripper," I stammered and half-waved at him before catching up to Taylor. Ripper just nodded.

We crossed the street and headed toward Taylor's building. A mattress was propped up against an old shell of a car. Used to be a Buick, I think. It had been there so long, I couldn't remember what the story was. Did someone own it, or did it just appear like so many other cars? But right now it was being used to hold up a mattress and some blankets, sheets, and clothes. Some crazy lady in Taylor's building threw them all out her window when she and her old man got into it. It wasn't the first time. Every time she and one of her boyfriends got into a fight, she would start hollering and carrying on, and finally she would throw all his stuff out the window. There were nights when I could hear her in my room, across the street. I don't know if other streets are like mine or if it's just U Street, but at night everything echoes. I hear very clearly someone kicking a can, clanking it along the street, cats fighting, cars honking, people yelling. And the crazy lady has a voice I got to know very well.

When we got to his building, Taylor stopped and sat on the front stoop. I sat next to him, and he pulled out two 20-dollar bills and a 10. He counted it out and waved it in front of me.

"Fifty bucks." He smiled. "It's the most money I ever had."

"Let's see." I held out my hand and made my first big mistake. Taylor put the money in my hand, and I counted it. Fifty dollars. It was the most money I had ever held. I thought about what I would do if it were mine. I would just walk into the kitchen and say, "Ma, I have a present for you. Don't go to work tonight," and I would hand her the money.

Ma works days, 8 a.m. to 4 p.m., in a hospital laundry. She works nights, 6 p.m. to midnight, in a fast-food restaurant. She makes $4.50 an hour. She doesn't even make $30 a night, and here I had $50. Taylor made $50 in about 30 minutes, and Ma works for six hours. I would walk right up to her and say—

"Ripper likes you," Taylor's voice broke into my dream. "He told me."

"How does he know?"

"What?"

"How does he know he likes me? He don't even know me."

"I dunno," Taylor shrugged. "I guess he likes what he sees. He asked me how you do in school and stuff. I guess he thinks you're real smart."

I handed Taylor back his money.

"Ripper's gonna be real big one day, and I'm gonna be with him. He's gonna take us all with him, man." Taylor kind of hit my arm. "You wait and see. People respect him. He's not like the others."

"That's not what I heard. I heard—" but he wouldn't let me finish.

"You gonna listen to people talk junk about him? You 'member when we couldn't even walk to the store?"

Taylor was right. Before Ripper stepped in, there were always different gangs fighting around the store at 14th Street. Not just the T-Posse. There were a few different ones taking up 14th Street. Like they were testing it out, trying to see if they could be a gang there. At first the fighting was just at night, but then things got so bad, you couldn't even go there in the middle of the day.

When Ripper came, he just laid down the law, and the fighting stopped. Some of those people just up and disappeared. T-Posse moved to 15th Street. I knew that Mr. Phillips, who ran the store, was very thankful. His business was going to be ruined 'cause no one could shop there. Ripper made sure that Mr. Phillips and his customers were safe. That's where my ma shops too. The word got around that Ripper killed a couple of gang members, but when the neighborhood was quiet again, most people didn't care how Ripper did it.

"Man, you let people dog him like that? He's takin' care of us." Taylor was protecting his new homeboy. I wasn't impressed.

"So, what you gonna do with the money?" I changed the subject. But I couldn't help thinking about the fact that it was gun money, drug money. People in my neighborhood were getting killed by guns and drugs every day, and here was Taylor helping the cause.

"Me and Brad are savin' up to buy a TV. A big one," and he put out his arms to show how big it was going to be.

"How much do you have?"

"This is it," and he put on a big smile. "We needed $40, and now we got it. We're gonna get it tomorrow."

"Cool," I said, smiling. Trying, anyway. I was trying to be happy for him, but I wasn't. Worse, I was kind of jealous. I just couldn't help but think if that was all Taylor had to do—carry a little brown bag around the street corner—I could have done that. Just one time, you know? For one time I could have bought my mama a night at home.

Grandma tells Ma about her TV stories. She tells Ma about who said what and how so-and-so is going to get even with so-and-so. Ma knows all the names and keeps up with the stories through Grandma. I would have loved to have her stay home one day and watch the stories with Grandma. I just about smiled imagining them together, talking during the commercials. Grandma gets so excited. She even starts talking to me about them. "Oooh, boy, did you hear that?" And then to the TV, "Oh, Lord, child, don't let him talk to you that way. Uh huh, that's right, honey. Mmm hmm, I heard that!"

And don't even remind her that they're just actors! She doesn't care that some lady down the street is throwing clothes out the window again; she just turns up the volume, scoots her chair a little closer to the set, and keeps talking to the people on the TV. She doesn't want to miss a word so later she can tell Ma all about it. It's funny 'cause Ma has to step over the mattress and clothes to get home, but all she hears about is how some lady on TV is in a coma and dying but popped out to wrestle a bear to the ground trying to save a beehive, or something crazy like that.

I don't know how long Taylor had been talking. His voice was like a buzz in the back of my head, but then I heard him say, "You should go tonight."

Maybe that was what made up my mind. Or maybe it was the way Ripper had shaken his head at me saying it was unfair that I could never see Ma. I'm not real sure. I can't make excuses. It's just that knowing that we already had a TV set but Ma could never watch it made my stomach hurt.

SIX

THEY call it "gettin' numbers." I heard that the mafia calls it "getting bones." It's when you kill someone. I had heard of the really rough gangs that require a new guy to "get bones" before he can become a full-fledged member of a gang. Would they make me "get bones"? I knew I could never do that. Or I could get jumped too. Taylor said it only lasts something like 30 seconds. But getting punched and beaten was nothing compared to shooting someone. Man, I was really nervous.

We headed down U, hung a right at the corner store, and walked down 14th for a while. A lot of people are afraid of 14th, but I like it. Something is always happening. There are lights at night and guys standing outside the clubs hollering for people to come watch their shows. Cars cruise up and down. The streets are filled with cabbies, trucks, and lots and lots of tourists. Maybe one or two cops. Most of the cops are down by the Capitol, though, keeping an eye out for the tourists. Once you get past P Street, people don't matter so much.

Taylor took me past 14th and V, down by the sewer system. Rows of old buildings, abandoned cars, trash, and a tree or two were all that was there. We slid down a small hill and went a couple of steps into a huge pipe. No one was paying any attention to us. We were standing under V Street. I had been there before when I was little, but I hadn't been in years because I knew that gangs hung out there.

When Taylor and I got into the pipe, a light flipped on. It was Gilly. He put a flashlight under his chin. The light came up on his face in a weird way, and he looked evil. He made an evil laugh on purpose. Even though I knew it was him, it still freaked me a little. Then he put the light down on us. There was enough light to see everyone. Gilly, Brad, Jackson, and four or five other guys that I really didn't know were standing there. The biggest surprise was Tommy Watson. He was a year younger than Taylor and me. Later, I found out that he had been a member for over a year. He was so quiet, I always figured he was kind of a nerd or something. It was a real surprise to find out that he was in a gang. Taylor told me that he was one of Ripper's favorite runners.

Gilly stepped forward and stood right in front of me.

"You got smart." He grinned.

"I guess so." I could feel myself squirming.

Jackson stepped up to me and sized me up. He stared hard at me.

"You say he's cool?" he asked Tommy. Tommy nodded. I felt funny. Here was this kid I thought was kind of a geek, and he was giving me the "okay." Jackson seemed to think I was okay if Tommy Watson said so, and he backed off a little. But Gilly was still eyeing me.

Taylor tried to vouch for me.

"He's cool. He's my best friend."

"Shut up, man, you're still on probation." Gilly's voice boomed out in the pipe, but his eyes never left me. "You see, you got to prove to us you trustworthy. We gotta know that you can be trusted and will never break the code." He looked at Taylor for a second. "Taylor has been doin' pretty good. He showed us that he can be trusted, but we like to be careful, you know."

Gilly looked at Jackson and spread his hands out as if he would like to let me in, but there was nothing he could do about it. "Tell you what; we got a run for you both. If you two can do it, you're in. Both of you. But if you screw it up . . ." He shrugged his shoulders and then made his hand like a gun and pretended to shoot us with his index finger. He was not smiling.

We had a job to do. The next day after school, instead of going home, we stayed on the bus and went to the corner of R and 15th. This was bad news. My stomach was in knots. We were stepping into the T-Posse territory. Ripper said it was okay because no one knew us. We were just two schoolboys, right? But all I knew about the T-Posse was that they didn't care who you were. Ripper told us just to look like we belonged and we'd be cool. We both had our books with us because we had a test the next day in social studies. We looked the "student" part. Before we went to Harriet E. Wilson, we never had books to carry home. Our school didn't have enough books for kids to take home; there were too many kids and not enough books. But ever since Taylor and I started going to Harriet E. Wilson, it seems like I'm always carrying books home. I like it now, but it was hard to get used to. I really didn't mind this time.

I took off my jacket and tied the books inside. I zipped up the zipper and used the sleeves to tie a knot. I put my arm through the tied sleeves and slung it over my shoulder like a back pack. Taylor did the same. We got off the bus and stood at the corner, waiting for our next set of instructions.

A girl we had never seen before came up to us and handed us a note. Taylor opened it up and read it. It told us to walk down to T Street.

"Man, that's bull," I said when I saw it. T and 15th was the T-Posse. Ripper was trying to get us killed!

"Let's go." Taylor acted like he was enjoying himself, like we were spies.

"Are you crazy? Did you see this?" I waved the note in front of him.

"Yeah, and we do like it says. We've got our books," Taylor wiggled the books that hung over his shoulder. He smiled, but I knew it was a front. He was as scared as me. "We do like Ripper says," he repeated himself.

"You know this is crazy. We're gonna get killed." I was shaking my head.

"It's a test. That's all. It's a test." He shrugged, trying harder than ever to look like it was no big deal.

"Yeah," I laughed, "you don't see Ripper here. Man, he don't even come down here. He's sending us to do his—"

"Hey," Taylor suddenly pointed a finger at me. "Do you want this or not, man? Do you want in?"

I stood on 15th, looking in the direction of T Street. It was funny how the neighborhoods could look all the same to someone—an outsider. To me, this neighborhood was very different from mine. Although the buildings were all the same drab color, an old yellow, these looked very different. I didn't recognize any lace curtains or old blankets tacked up. I saw some mini blinds, cream-colored curtains, some bare windows, and some broken ones.

"Do you want in?" he asked again. No. No, I didn't. Not for this. But my feet started walking. I started to move toward T Street. I wasn't thinking or talking; I was just looking. There were about a dozen people outside. Two or three sat on front stoops, stoops that crumbled from age and excess use. Cement crumbled away and made perfect throwing rocks for kids. Up the street, some man was yelling for his dog. His whistles bounced off the building and echoed like at U, but it was different. It seemed more eerie, vacant. My feet kept walking.

When we got to the corner of 15th and T, there was a kid about our age standing there. He was staring at us while we were walking to the corner, so I figured he was our contact. That, or he was going to whip out a piece and blow us away. He never said a word; he just walked up and handed me a little box. My heart was pounding. He turned and disappeared into a laundromat that was across the street. I looked at Taylor. He watched the kid for a second and then took the box and read the instructions. It told us to go to the pipe. Without a word, we turned and walked back to the pipe.

"It's another test," Taylor breathed as we turned our backs to T Street. No T-Posse. We picked up our pace almost to a run.

We slipped down the hill that was partially fenced off. Someone had cut the fencing and pulled it back. We hung on the end of the fence and hopped down to the cement floor just in front of the pipe. It was pitch black inside the pipe, but we had the light from outside, so we stood on the very edge so we could see each other. I started to reach out for the box when I heard the noise. I jerked my head up in time to see two big guys jump in front of the pipe. They had come from the top of it. The jump was farther than they'd thought because they both stumbled for a moment. The looks on their faces told me they were bad news.

As soon as they stood up, I took off running. Taylor was right behind me. The guys had blocked off the entrance, so we ran down the pipe. It didn't take more than 20 steps before we were in complete darkness. There was a little water—or whatever it was—on the bottom of the pipe. I didn't care what it was; it had to be better than what was chasing us. The splashing of our feet was the only noise I could hear. It was really hard to run in total darkness. I guess I kept slowing down because I could feel Taylor's hand on my back from time to time. I kept thinking I was going to trip over something. Then I heard a thud, and Taylor swore. We kept running.

A moment later, I felt his hand on my shirt. He was stopping me. We stopped and listened. We could hear splashing. They were still coming. Taylor felt along the walls and pulled me into another pipe. He knew his way pretty well in there. We took a few more steps, and he pulled me down so that we both slid against the wall into a squat position. We both steadied our breathing so they couldn't hear us. The sounds got closer and closer. Everything got quiet for a minute, and then I heard someone's voice.

"Get the light."

A light flipped on, and I could see huge shadows from where we were sitting. They grew bigger and bigger. I could feel Taylor breathe in as they neared the edge of our tunnel. At that moment, a light flashed in my eyes. I was blinded. I put up my hand to block the light, but it was grabbed, and I was yanked to my feet. The flashlight was pushed in my face. Taylor was pulled out too.

"Give me the box," a voice demanded.

"What box?" Taylor's voice trembled.

"The box, the box!" The voice was yelling at us. He wasn't playing games.

"Look, I don't got a box." Taylor sounded like he was going to cry. Then I felt someone grab me again.

"Give me the box!" I was being shaken.

"All I got is my books," and I slid the jacket filled with my books off my shoulders. "That's all I got, my books."

"Look, just give me the box, and you won't get hurt." The voice sounded familiar to me. Before I could say another word, I was hit. All I knew was that one second I was breathing just fine and the next second I could barely breathe. I caught a fist in the gut. The pain was incredible. I doubled over, vaguely hearing myself make some kind of "woof" sound. A second blow came, and my knees buckled, but the fisted hand held onto my shirt, holding me up. I flopped around like a rag doll, trying to catch my breath. I felt like I was going to black out. I was seeing stars, and my stomach was on fire.

The voice demanded the box again, and

that's when I realized this was it. I was getting tested and jumped at the same time. Two, three more hits came, but it didn't matter. It hurt. It hurt a lot, but it's not so bad when you know it's not going to kill you.

"I told you. I don't got a box," I managed to say. "All I got is my books." I was coughing. The pain was doubling me over. The hand let me drop to the ground, and I crouched over the sewer water. That's what it was. Only two inches from the water, I could smell its awful stench, but I couldn't move. It would take several minutes before I could move again.

There was silence for a moment, then a short laugh. It was Ripper.

"Not bad."

"Hey, who . . . ?" Taylor was so scared, it had taken him a minute to realize this was our test. Taylor had already been jumped. He hadn't thought it would happen to me when I was with him. He had been scared for his life.

"I gotta know that if I give you something, you won't just go turning it over if someone scares you. Not bad!" Compliments from Ripper were hard to come by. I guess I was kind of proud when he slapped me on the back. I staggered to my feet, holding my stomach.

"So, where's the box?"

"I threw it in the hole you showed me," Taylor answered, and Gilly flashed his light over the wall of the pipe. There was a small hole on the side. Gilly walked over and pulled out the box. Ripper flashed his light back on Taylor. He reached forward and patted the side of his face. Another compliment.

"This one's for real," and he handed me an envelope. "Take it to the store and give it to Mr. Phillips." I looked at Taylor and nodded. "No, Taylor, you stay with me. Steve, when you drop it off, go home. I'll see you later."

I took the envelope and started to walk out of the pipe when Ripper called after me, "And no peekin'!" The light was under his face, and he looked like a monster. I nodded my head and started toward the store. It took me forever to climb back up the hill from the pipe. My stomach was burning hot. But after several minutes, I made it up and headed for the store, limping the whole way.

After that day, Ripper gave me and Taylor things to run every now and then. The first time I took the envelope to Mr. Phillips, he looked really funny. He was as surprised to see me make the delivery as I was that he was taking them. I think he was embarrassed or something. He liked my ma a lot. What would she say if she knew he was involved with Ripper? What would she say if she knew I was involved with Ripper? I tried not to think too much about that last part. I had figured out on my own that Mr. Phillips was just the "middle man." He allowed his store to be used as a drop-off point. I guess he figured he owed Ripper for saving his business or maybe Ripper had something on him. Anyway, the store was where I did most of my runs.

I saved up $400 in a month. It's funny, but once I started making the money, I couldn't decide what to do with it. And I never really felt that bad about running errands for Ripper, even though I knew it was drug money. I blocked it out of my head. I was fooling myself. But once I had all that money, I had a problem. I knew that if I bought something for Ma or just gave it to her, she would want to know where it came from. So I just kept quiet and saved it all.

Taylor and I had become full members. Ripper had given us both blue bandannas. To some, maybe that's not such a great gift, but from Ripper, it was a symbol. You couldn't wear a bandanna unless it was given to you. I'd been jumped, passed the test, and kept the goods on my homeboys. I was as good as any of them. At first, I had joined thinking I could help Ma, but I got to like Ripper and Jackson. They were real cool. It was hard to believe any of the bad stuff I heard about them. Ripper just wanted to make the neighborhood good again. And he had felt real bad about punching me too. But he had to know if I could take it, you know? He didn't want to, but he had to test me. He said that we had some of the good things in life coming to us, and we were going to get them. It was like he wanted the same things that Malcolm X had wanted. And neither of them was afraid to talk about it. Ripper wanted the people of our neighborhood to have a good life. He was right. Ma worked so hard, and for nothing. Ripper would change all that. For a while, it seemed like a dream come true.

SEVEN

Mr. Peterson kept his word and found us a book to read about Malcolm X. It talked about where he was born, how the KKK terrorized his family, and how he got shuffled around from home to home when he was young. More than the first half of the book told about what a bad life he had, and it made me mad.

The things in the book were like the way things were on the streets near my neighborhood. Things hadn't changed that much. It made me think about how some kids had called me "nigger" when I first came to Harriet E. Wilson, and it made me think about how really screwed up things are in this country. I could understand Ripper better and better.

People talk about how poor people don't try to help themselves, how they're lazy and stuff, but no one ever gives the poor people a chance to make things better. The cops don't care about me. The teachers at my last school didn't really care, either. It wasn't that they were creeps or anything, but they didn't have the books, the supplies, or the time to give us. They were so mad at the schools that they just didn't have time for us. The politicians are always arguing for the power, and they don't care about me or any other poor people. It's the same stuff. What Malcolm X was mad about, I was too.

I told Ripper what the *X* stood for one day when he was wearing his hat.

"It's to symbolize freedom," I said, and Ripper got a grin on his face. "Little was his real last name, but he believed that Little was the name given to his family when they were slaves. Malcolm didn't like the idea of having a slave name, but he didn't know what his name was when his people were taken from Africa, so he used *X*. *X* stands for his African name." I got all that from my book.

"See what I mean? This schoolboy is smart," Ripper said to Jackson and Little Tommy. "I got to keep you around so you can educate me," he laughed. And I felt real good.

In class, it was different. All the other kids just thought Malcolm X was too mean, that he hated all whites for no reason. They all agreed that there were some whites who were bad, but that there were whites who were nice too. Everyone kept coming back to Martin Luther

King and saying how he tried to do things the right way, but those kids didn't live in my neighborhood. They didn't have to worry about their mamas late at night, and they knew the police weren't afraid to drive on their streets. They couldn't understand.

They all had real good lives. They had their pony-riding classes, soccer, or baseball after school. We didn't have playing fields where I lived. And there was definitely no place for a horse. Those kids all lived in those big, white houses I saw every morning when our bus pulled into the school's neighborhood. They had dishwashers and washing machines. I bet their mamas could watch their stories if they wanted. And I bet they knew where their fathers were.

Sundays were the best at my house. Ma didn't have to work on Sundays, so we got to spend the whole day together and eat dinner together like a regular family. In the summertime, we didn't use the stove because it made the house too hot, but in the winter, it was great. The kitchen would be all warm and toasty, and we would all huddle together and talk about stuff—even talking about Grandma's stories was fun. Sometimes I felt bad for Taylor. Even when his mama was there, it was like she wasn't there at all. It's too bad Taylor couldn't have a mama like Ma.

It's kind of a family joke that the stove talks too. It makes popping noises long after it's turned off. Sometimes its timing is perfect. Grandma will be going on about something, asking, "Am I right? Well, am I right?" *POP!* It makes Ma mad. She's called and called to get someone to fix it, but the housing folks have better things to do. Anything but come out our way. Everytime it pops, she sighs, but I like it. It's just part of the house, part of some of the noises I listen to at night.

Most nights I didn't fall asleep until I heard Ma come through the front door. I would lie awake thinking of things, like how I wished she didn't have to work and come home so late. I used to try to think up ways to rob a bank or a drugstore. Not 'cause of the thrill of it, like some guys I know. I would steal just enough to let Ma stay home, or maybe even just enough so that she would only have to work one job. I would never hurt anyone, just take enough and go. No one would ever catch me because I would wear a great disguise. I had it figured out too—I would dress up like a woman. I would take one of Ma's bras and stuff it, wear a dress, and put on sunglasses and lipstick. I knew it would work, and no one would ever suspect it was a 13-year-old boy because no way would any guy in the whole world do something like that. At least, no guy from U Street.

I always heard Ma come in the front door, and she and Grandma would talk in low tones to not wake me. It's a small apartment with thin walls, so I can hear almost everything. Sometimes I would catch every other word. Ma would tell Grandma about work at first. She hated her night job. Her boss was a kid, like 20 years younger than Ma, and I knew he didn't treat her so well. He talked down to her, like he was better than her. It embarrassed her. He was in high school, and she has a boy who's almost there. But this guy, this boss of hers, reminded her all the time that he knew plenty of kids at his school who would love to have her job. She was afraid to ever ask for nights off. She told Grandma that he would replace her in a heartbeat.

Then Grandma would tell Ma about something I did or said, and then about her stories. I could always tell from Ma's voice that she really liked to hear about that stuff. It was something they could gossip about, have fun about, a fantasy—like mine about robbing a bank.

And always there was the *pop! pop!* from the kitchen. Somehow it added to their talk.

Sometimes Ma ignored it, but sometimes it made her mad and she would swear "come heaven or high water" the stove would be fixed. She complained about her salary and the housing, but sometimes that little *pop! pop!* would get her to talking about my father. I didn't know much. Didn't care. She'd say it was his fault we're here, that he left us here, that the only good thing that ever came of him was me. No matter how mad she was, it always came to that. *The only good that came from my father was me.* I'd fall asleep listening to Ma and Grandma's voices, laughing about one of the characters on one of the shows. "Ooooh, can you believe that? And then what?"

After I started running with the Jags, I'd lie in bed at night and think about my great disguise and Malcolm X. The more I tried to understand Malcolm X, the more I thought that Martin Luther King was too quiet. He was too nice. "Nice guys finish last" is the way I always heard it.

But as time wore on, I started to notice things that weren't right. There were some things I just couldn't ignore.

EIGHT

Taylor changed a lot during those months after we joined the Jags. At first, when we jumped in, it had been exciting. We made money, and the deliveries were kind of like top secret FBI stuff. Ripper seemed to really care about us. But the more I was around, the more he said things I didn't like.

Ma always told me that she was sick and tired of listening to people who always complained about "being down" but were never willing to do honest, hard work. She said Ripper was a con artist. He always got other kids to do his dirty work for him, and he was always making excuses. It was always someone else's fault that he didn't have an education or that he didn't have this or that.

Taylor had started doing the same stuff. He started saying things about the Koreans who owned stores in our neighborhood. He said things about his mother's boss 'cause he was white. It was weird that I had always thought that white people were prejudiced but had never thought that my friend, Taylor, would get that way.

I didn't like it. I had understood why Malcolm X said the things he did, but that was different. Taylor was spoiled compared to the way Malcolm X grew up. Still, I was at the point in my book where Malcolm had joined a religion, the Nation of Islam. To understand the religion better, he took a trip to Mecca. That is the holiest of the holy places where Muslims worship. But when he got there it was just like Ma had said. He saw how blacks and whites all got along together, and the white people in other countries just loved him. They all thought he was a great speaker and wanted to hear him. Malcolm X realized that he had been wrong and wanted to be able to live in harmony like the people in Mecca.

He began to reconsider things that he had said about Martin Luther King and wanted to change his ways. It made me rethink things too—like Ripper and Taylor.

I didn't like the way Ripper pushed people, and I didn't like that I was helping him move drugs and who knows what else. About a week before the kid came into our neighborhood, I told Taylor I was going to quit. The next day, I got a visit from Ripper. I found out that people can't just "quit" his gang.

"Man, I don't get you. You got a good thing goin' here. Why you want to mess all that up?" Ripper shook his head at me. I didn't say a word.

"See, you worried that you with a gang, but it ain't a gang, man. We're brothers. We're like family. And I take care of my family. You know? Take your mama. She work late hours, and these streets are dangerous. Because she's your ma, she part of our family. We'll look out for her. No one'll mess with her. The word is out." He was staring at me while he talked, but I just stared straight ahead. We were sitting on the stoop outside my building. I worked my heel on the edge of the stoop, breaking away some of the cement.

"I like your ma. She's a nice-looking lady. I don't wanna see her get hurt, you know?"

I didn't like the way he kept bringing up my mama. I wasn't stupid. I knew what he was all about. I knew that he was trying to scare me into staying.

"I ain't gonna say anything to anyone if that's what you think," I said finally. He shook his head as though it had never come to his mind, but I knew that was what he was afraid of. I knew too much. He tried to bring up Malcolm X because he knew I was really into him. Ripper tried to remind me what Malcolm X had said. It was them against us. Like I said, I'm not stupid, and neither was he.

I didn't think I had much of a choice, so I told him that I would stay. I thought that if I could just get him off my back, it would all blow over. But he had decided to give me more runs. The more I was in it, the harder it would be to get out.

I had picked up a bag from the store and taken it to a block I had never been to before. It was up past W Street. There used to be government housing up there, but the houses were closed down. The buildings were so overrun with roaches and rats, the health department shut the buildings down and kicked everyone out. The row houses were under partial construction and had been for what seemed forever. So, they just sat there—abandoned, broken-down, and perfect for the kind of deals Ripper made.

I reread the address on the bag. When I was about halfway into the block, I found the address. It was right in the middle of the other buildings. The windows had all been broken long ago. A door hung on only the top hinges, so it looked like something from a ghost town in a

Western. I looked around before I went up the front steps. I knew that nothing would happen to me. I knew that Ripper liked me and would always look out for me, but something was spooking me. Maybe because it was a different neighborhood. Maybe. Or maybe it was that this neighborhood was a lot like mine, only too quiet. Knowing that I was stepping into an abandoned building where no one could hear me or help me if I got into trouble gave me the creeps. I stopped on the bottom step and looked around again.

There were a few cars on the streets; one was stripped clean. Two other cars were in perfect condition. One of them had tinted windows. It wasn't a Mercedes or anything, but it was pretty nice to be sitting around. That just wasn't right. Cars like that don't last too long in my neighborhood. Why would something like that be here? And there was something else—there were no kids on the street. No skip rope, no ball, no nothing. The neighborhood had been shut down, but still guys used to come up here all the time to play ball and stuff. I looked back at the building. At the top of the steps there was a bum. He was just sitting there with his booze. I stared at him for a second. It was all too much. It was like my block, but there was no kind of life anywhere.

I told myself that I was just letting my imagination get to me, and I walked up the steps past the bum. As I passed him, I looked down and saw the scariest thing in the world. Behind the folds of his coat, I could see what looked like the top part of a walkie talkie. I practically tripped into the stairwell. He never looked at me. He just kept chattering to himself like he was crazy, but I knew that he was acting. He was a cop, and this was a setup! I was supposed to walk up the stairs and deliver the package, and then everyone would be busted.

My mind was flying a hundred miles an hour. The stairs were off to the left of the narrow hallway. Straight ahead, there was a back door. Most times, these doors are blocked off by the landlords even though they're supposed to be fire exits. This door had been blocked off at one time, but someone had pulled the bars away from the frame. Two metal bars kind of stuck straight out where they had been pulled. There was just enough room for me to slip through.

I peeked over my shoulder at the cop and then took off. If I wasn't sure before, I knew then. The second I took off, the cop yelled out and jumped to his feet. By the time he was standing, I was through the door. I jumped down the back stairs and started to run. I knew that if this was really a bust, there would be a ton of cops around. I stuffed the envelope into my pants and jumped at a fence that stood on the other side of the alley.

Behind the building was the oldest part of the hood. It had been abandoned even before I was born, but about two or three years ago the city put a fence around the whole area. It's too dangerous for any kids to be climbing on. On the other side of the old neighborhood is the block connected to mine. I knew that if I could just get through there, I could be home real fast and the cops would never find me. I was so scared, the only thing that went through my mind was to run!

I could hear the bum—the cop. He had broken through another bar and was coming down the stairs after me. Down the alley, the car that had been sitting on the street came swinging into sight. I climbed the chain-link fence and jumped over it. I hit the ground and headed for an old building. I planned to do the same thing I had done at the other building. I would run up the stairs, cut down the hallway, and slip out the back. Once I got to the other side of the building, they would lose sight of me, and I could make it home. As I headed for the old building, I heard the clinking of the fence again. I looked over my shoulder and saw three cops on the fence. My heart stopped.

I sprang onto the steps and ran into the building.

"STOP!"

Too late. I ran inside. The second I made it into the building, the floor gave out. I never really knew that I was falling. I just had this really weird sensation in my stomach, and then my back felt real hot. Everything was dark. I landed hard and got the wind knocked out of me for a couple of minutes. I lay there holding my chest and trying to breathe when I heard their voices.

"He made it through," I heard one voice say.

"All right, call in. Get someone to swing around the other side. Maybe we can pick him up there," another voice said.

I heard some more mumbles and then a sharp laugh like someone had just discovered something really great.

"Thank you!" I heard a voice call out. I could tell it was meant for me.

Thank you?

I kept perfectly still. I didn't know what they meant by that. I didn't care. Finally, my breath came back. The fall had really hurt, but once I was able to breathe comfortably again, I realized it was my back that was hurting. I reached behind me and felt the wetness. I was bleeding badly. When the cops' voices faded away, I stood and tried to figure a way out. I guess they figured I'd jumped over the hole. They never thought to look down and see if I had fallen in.

A little light came in through the hole, and I was able to see some wood leaning on the side of the wall where I was. I climbed up the wood like a ladder. When I got to the top, I poked my head out and looked around to see if the coast was clear. I slipped through the hole and sneaked around the back of the building. To be safe, I waited for about an hour, or what seemed like an hour. Then I climbed over the fence and ran.

Once I cleared the abandoned area, I stood, bent over, catching my breath in an open lot. I patted my belt to check the envelope. My heart fell, and I began wildly patting myself all over, even places I knew it couldn't be. It was gone! It was gone! That's what the "thank you" was for. When I had climbed over the fence, the envelope had fallen out, and now the cops had it. My mind ran a million miles an hour, but only on the same thing—the package was gone. Gone!

Suddenly I thought of Ripper. *Oh, my God!* What would I tell Ripper? I stood up and threw my hands up to my face, covering my eyes. If ever there was a time I thought about crying, this was it. I began to pace. Maybe I could go back. But what would be the point? The cops had the envelope. They had told me so. They had it, and I didn't. What was I going to tell Ripper?

I bent over in a half-squat position, hands over my face, thinking, Oh, my God. I'm a dead man. My back was throbbing, but it didn't matter. Nothing mattered. I couldn't go home. I couldn't go back. But where could I go? All I could do was stand there in an empty lot.

Somewhere off in the distance, I could hear sirens. So I couldn't stay there much longer. It would only be minutes before some cops might come by just to see if the kid was still around. The cops who had chased me would be able to recognize me, and standing there bleeding, it would be a little hard to claim innocence. I had to go *somewhere*.

I headed home.

When I turned the corner coming up my block, I could see Ripper and a bunch of the others standing around my stoop. Ripper looked tense. He had his hands shoved in his pockets and was motionless. He was staring me down hard. Taylor was smiling.

"See, he made it. I told you," I heard Taylor saying as I got closer. "Hey, man, we heard a bust went down."

"It did," I said and looked at Ripper. He never moved.

"What happened?" Taylor moved toward me.

"Where's the envelope?" Gilly stepped up very close to me.

I just stood there. I could feel a hot streak of sweat coming down my face. I hoped they wouldn't notice since I was covered in sweat and dirt.

"I'm not talkin' to you 'cause I think you're good-lookin'," Gilly said, moving in real close to my face. Little Tommy Watson laughed at this, but Ripper scowled. There was nothing funny about what was going to be said. He sensed that.

"I don't got it," I said under Gilly's gaze. It was piercing.

"You don'—" Gilly started, but Ripper stepped down off the last step, shoving Gilly to the side, and moved in real close to me. His voice was barely a whisper.

"What you mean, you don't got it?"

"I lost it," I choked.

There was this kind of gasp from everyone. It was one of those TV story moments. Everyone was frozen; no one could or would talk. They were waiting for the commercial. They were waiting for Ripper. He drew in a deep breath and studied me hard. I never took my eyes off him. I didn't move.

"So, what went down?" He finally spoke.

I told him how the wino was a cop, how I broke away from the back of the building and outran them but must have lost the envelope going over the fence. I tried to tell Ripper that the only reason I ran was so they *wouldn't* get the package, but he seemed to know that.

"My man evaded the cops and ripped up his back, and he ain't even crying about it." He faced everyone, his face breaking out into a smile. The guys backed off me a little, but they were uncertain. Like me, it was hard to figure Ripper out. Was he okay with this, really? Or was he going to get me later? He squeezed my shoulders and started to walk me down the street.

"We'll just have to make it up in double-time," he called back to Gilly, who just stood there motionless. Ripper stopped and looked back at everyone. No one had moved.

"Hey, this is family business, right?" There was an edge to his voice. Gilly and Little Tommy nodded halfheartedly.

When we started to walk, I felt Ripper's grip tighten slightly on my shoulder. His voice was very deep and clear.

"How much you figure was in that package?" he asked me. I shrugged. I didn't know. I never looked. It was one thing I never did—I never peeked. He nodded, acting like a patient father. "About $1,200. That's a lot to lose in one afternoon, my man. But," he threw up his hand in protest, "that's okay, you know? You my main man. You the one who's gonna educate me, right?" He laughed at this like it was a good joke. "Now, it don't do me no good to be mad at you. You did your best. You was smart to see through that cop. But," he let his voice drop again, "you lost something very valuable. Now, I know you don't have that kind of bread lyin' around."

"I have $400 saved up," I said meekly. "I can pay you back."

"Oh, I know you will," he said, and there was a certain amount of pleasure in his voice. "You know I like you, right?" I nodded. My heart was beginning to sink again. I now owed Ripper $800. I was never going to get out of the Jags. Ripper would hold this over me. There was no getting out, and it made him happy as could be.

Ripper took me to a clinic and paid the doctor to stitch me up. I got ten stitches, and Ripper paid for the whole thing. Afterwards, he bought me a cheeseburger and fries and walked me home again. He kept telling me how proud he was of me and how glad he was to have me back in the family.

NINE

WHEN I got home, dinner was waiting for me. I couldn't tell Grandma that Ripper had bought me dinner, so I just told her that I wasn't hungry and went to my room. When Ma got home, she knocked on my door. I wanted to tell her about the money and what had happened today. But if I told her that I had delivered an envelope filled with money to buy drugs off an undercover cop and almost got caught, she would kill me. It would break her heart. How was I supposed to tell her about Mr. Phillips and his store? I knew better. Why was I so stupid? The whole reason all this started in the first place was because of her stupid jobs, but now none of that mattered. I was in too deep with Ripper now. I was in, and it had nothing to do with Ma or her jobs.

I told her to come in. "You feel okay, baby?" She was frowning at me.

"Yeah," I shrugged my shoulders. "I'm just not hungry, that's all." I peeked at her.

"You sure? You feel a little warm." She always thinks I feel too warm. She worries too much about me. I know she feels bad because she isn't around that much. So when she is, she is all over me.

"You always say that," I tried to smile, but it didn't work.

"No, I don't." She tweaked my nose. "But I know how you are. You won't tell me if you don't feel well so I won't worry. And it doesn't work that way. I worry no matter what you do. I'm a mother." And she smiled and rubbed my head. She sure was pretty when she smiled like that.

"I just wish you didn't have to work so much."

"Me too, baby," and her hand fell a little. "I wish I could be here with you, but we got bills. We got to eat."

"What if I worked?" I raised my eyebrows at her.

"You? No way! You already have a job." She shook her head.

"What?"

"You go to school and take care of your grandma."

"Ma . . ." I started to shake my head. That was crazy.

Pop!

I smiled and Ma frowned at the exact same time. She caught my smile and matched it.

"Now, why do you find that funny?" She sounded exasperated.

"Because," I grinned, "it is. It makes you so mad, but it's been doin' it for so long. I don't know why you care."

"It's just another thing. It's one more thing I got to worry about. Lord help us all if it just explodes one day!"

"It's not going to explode." I laughed out loud.

"Not before you get us out of here when you become a famous doctor," she punched me in the chest, and I fell back on the bed.

"A famous doctor?"

Her eyes were shining. When she smiled at me, she was prettier than Ms. Whitley. Every kid should have a mama like Ma. She is just so sweet, it's hard to understand why my father walked out. How could he do that? But, like I say, I don't care about that too much. I'm real happy with Ma and Grandma. Ma's eyes caught my journal.

"No, a famous writer. That's what you're going to be." She reached for the journal like she was going to read it. I jumped forward and snatched it from her reach. I didn't want her reading my thoughts.

"Ma, you talkin' crazy. I need to be working, to help you. That's how we're—" I wasn't smiling anymore, but neither was Ma.

"No," she raised her voice. "Now, I don't want to hear any more. You have to get good grades in school. You are going to college and be smart and will make a success of yourself. You think I'm working two jobs because I love to work?" She poked me in the stomach with her finger. "I'm working to save up for you. You're going to go to college and get a real job."

"But I could make money too. I could help you. Mama, you don't have to work so hard."

"Oh, yes I do. You think I want you to stay around here? Have you grow up to be like Ripper? No, I got bigger plans for you."

"He's not that bad," I said, but I wasn't sure I believed that.

"Boy, don't you pay attention? Ripper is no better than the other punks. He has some people fooled that he is a good guy because he stopped the violence on our streets, but he makes violence on other people's streets. I work with a lady who knows a kid who was killed because of Ripper and his gang." She shook her head. "He doesn't fool me. He's a bad one."

"Malcolm X used to be bad," I said. I'm not really sure what my point was, but I wanted to say it. Ma nodded her head.

"Not bad. Misinformed. But then he straightened himself out." She looked around the room until she saw my Malcolm X book and walked over to it. She picked it up and examined the front and back covers. "You know, I can't tell you how glad I am you're reading this, about him," and she tapped the picture of his face. "Now you understand more about what Grandma and I were saying." She looked at his picture again. "He was a strong, powerful man. He could have been a great leader for us."

"After he came back from Mecca?" I asked, but I already knew the answer. Ma had always taught me that violence never solved anything. She is more in thinking with Dr. King.

"After Mecca. He and Martin Luther King . . ." Her voice kind of disappeared, but I could tell her mind was going a mile a minute. She is a big fan of Dr. Martin Luther King. I guess she thought Malcolm X was okay too, toward the end.

She looked back at me and caught me studying her face.

"Ripper and kids like him are destroying everything Dr. King and Malcolm X wanted.

The drugs, the guns, the gangs—it's killing us, and it's killing 'The Dream.'"

I knew about "The Dream." It was Dr. Martin Luther King's, and he shared it with the world from the steps of the Lincoln Memorial in Washington, D.C. Ma had read it to me before. It's about a dream he had where one day all people would be treated equal no matter what their religion or race was. Maybe it doesn't sound that great, but to hear the whole speech is unlike anything in the world. And I always wondered what people who were prejudiced thought when they heard that speech because it is so great. I wonder how they couldn't like it.

Pop!

Ma ignored the pop this time.

"But," and she leaned forward and kissed my cheek, "as long as there are kids like you, I don't have to worry. You'll set things right!" She smiled and tried to tuck me in. She keeps trying to do that. I guess she doesn't realize that kids my age don't get tucked in anymore, so I squirmed around. She laughed, threw her hands up, and backed out of the room. She flipped off the light, and for a moment all I could see was the outline of her body. Then she closed the door and left me to think about what she had said.

Some kid I was, I thought. I'm the one who's supposed to set things right, and I'm running away from the police and taking money—blood money—from Ripper. Malcolm X had been bad once, I tried to tell myself. Then I remembered that he had landed in jail too. I knew that I had to get out of this mess before it was too late.

❊ ❊ ❊

I was on the basketball courts when Taylor found me.

"What's up with you?" he asked. He sounded a little annoyed.

"What do you mean?" I asked, and I took a shot at the basket. I was Michael Jordan, flying through the air.

"Ripper says that he can't get you to do any runs. Says every time he asks, you got something else you gotta do." He was eyeing me hard while I pretended to be one-on-one with Charles Barkley. I faked to the right, then the left. He was on me. I backed up, between the legs, spun around, and let it fly off to the left. Missed.

"I know for a fact that you haven't been doin' nothin'," he continued.

"No," I panted, "I've been doin' stuff for my

grandma." I shot and missed again. It was true I hadn't been doing anything. I just needed some time away to think. I knew I couldn't keep running with the Jags, but I couldn't get out of it. I owed too much money. I was in too deep to get out. I took a shot and missed. "You know, I could do a lot better if you weren't yappin' at me."

Taylor stepped in and played against me. He hunched over to block against me and kept talking.

"You act like you forgot everything Ripper's done for you," and he dove forward and slapped the ball out of my hands.

I hadn't forgotten what Ripper had done for me. So far, he had given me a lot of money, but I almost got caught by the police too. I nearly killed myself falling in that old building. I hadn't forgotten anything. And Ripper was reminding me daily. I covered Taylor pretty tight, and he bounced the ball off my foot by accident. I caught it, raced around Taylor, and sunk one in. Air Jordan was back!

Taylor was covering me again.

"He paid for your stitches and even bought you dinner," he lunged forward. I dodged him and tried to dribble around him.

"Yeah, I almost got killed." I took a shot and missed. Taylor watched the ball fall for a second and then turned to me. I was standing there with my hands on my hips, panting.

"I can't believe you dumped it, man. Man, you just lucky Ripper didn't tear you up," he said and shook his head like it was the craziest thing he'd ever heard.

"Don't worry about it. I'm payin' it back." Swoosh.

"You the one who wanted money to give your mama, and now you complainin'. Man, I don't get you. You can't just use Ripper when you need him and throw him out when you don't. Family don't act like that."

I stopped dribbling and looked at him.

"Is that you talkin' or Ripper? I can't tell anymore."

I started to play again, and Taylor rushed in and slapped the ball from my hands, only he didn't try to recover the ball. He was looking straight at me. I could hear the ball bounce a few times, but I stared right back at Taylor.

"This how it is? You gonna turn your back on everyone?"

Taylor had been my friend all my life, but things had changed. He wasn't the same. Everything was for Ripper, and he didn't seem to care that much about anyone else. I wanted to tell him about my ma and how she felt about

Ripper. But I could tell that whatever I told Taylor would go right back to Ripper, so I let it drop. I just shrugged my shoulders and turned around to get the ball again.

"He should have let you bleed then," and he stepped forward and slapped me on the back. It stung. It really stung. The stitches were just healing, but that felt like he tore them open again. I wheeled around and slugged him. Full on the mouth. It knocked him down, and he sat on the concrete and stared up at me holding his mouth. I had never hit Taylor or anyone before. He just sat there and stared at me, and I picked up the ball and walked back to the school.

After school, I took the bus home alone. I don't know where Taylor was. When he came back to class, he wouldn't look at me. When the bell rang, he disappeared. I waited for him for a while but never saw him.

The whole ride home I thought about how much Taylor had changed, but I realized I had changed too. If someone would have told me that I would hit Taylor, I would have laughed. No way would I ever hit him. He'd been my best friend all my life. But things weren't the same anymore. He wasn't the same anymore. I had always thought that Brad was kind of a jerk because he was always trying so hard to be someone he wasn't.

Now Taylor was the same way, and he worshipped the ground Ripper walked on. But I knew that if Taylor ever got caught running a bag, Ripper would never admit to the police or anyone that it was his. He'd let Brad, Taylor, Gilly, or all of us rot in jail. I didn't think he'd ever hurt us, but he sure wouldn't help us.

When I got home, I was surprised to see Ma was home. She and Grandma were sitting together by the front door. They were waiting for me. At first, for just a second, I was real happy to see her, but then I knew something was wrong. My eyes fell a little when I set down my books and saw my little box in Ma's hands. That was where I kept all the money. I looked back at Ma and then Grandma. They were waiting to hear my story.

"Hi," I started slow. I wasn't sure what to do. I was caught.

"Do you want to explain this to me?" Ma held up the box and let it fall again in her lap. Grandma didn't say a word.

"I've been working," I cleared my throat, "to save money so you could quit your job."

"Where?" She shook her head. "Where did you get this kind of money? There is over $400 here. Don't you lie to me. I want the truth. Where did you get this kind of money?"

I think four million years passed before I answered. It felt like I stared at her for a long time before I found the courage to tell her. I came straight out with it too. I told her that I had heard that Ripper paid kids a lot of money to run errands for him, so I joined up. When I said that, both Ma and Grandma gasped. I could tell that they had talked about it and had probably guessed that, but they had to hear it from me. When I actually said it out loud, it must have sounded much worse than just thinking it. Grandma began to shake her head, and Ma called me over to her. She took my hands and looked so hard into my eyes. I couldn't remember ever being stared at so hard.

"Do you know what you're doing? You're killing us."

"Huh?"

"You're killing us. Every time you help someone like Ripper bring drugs, drug money, or guns into our neighborhoods, you are killing us."

"No. No, Ma. Ripper is the one who cleaned everything up." I didn't really believe that, but it sounded better than me killing people. "He's doing it for our people."

"Listen, every time he gets his hands on drugs or a gun, he turns around and sells it to someone else. Those drugs and those guns go in and out of our neighborhoods, and people are killing one another left and right. It isn't just the black neighborhoods either. Latinos are killing blacks, and blacks are killing Latinos. Blacks are killing one another and white people, and white people are killing blacks. It moves in a vicious cycle. It just goes around and around, killing more and more innocent people." And she began to cry.

"What's a vicious cycle?" I asked.

"We live here because we're poor. Because we're poor, we can't afford to have good schools in our neighborhoods. Because our school system is bad, many children drop out and never get an education. They can't get good jobs because they don't have a good education, and after a while they stop trying to find jobs. They get depressed. They get poorer and poorer, and some people get desperate and commit crimes. Still, other people like Ripper don't even try in the first place, and they live off of other people's hard work. *That* is a vicious cycle." Ma looked up at me with tears in her eyes. "That is why it is so important for you to stay in school and learn. Maybe you can be the one who will come back to your neighborhood and make things better." She squeezed my arms a little and then looked back at the money. "And this, this is blood money," and she dropped the box on the floor.

I never told her that Mr. Phillips was involved. That would have really hurt her. She was feeling pretty good after I swore that I would quit the gang and have nothing more to do with the Jags. There was just one really big problem—I owed Ripper $1,200.

I had told Ma everything else, but I just couldn't tell her I was nearly busted by the cops up at W Street. It would have been too much for her and Grandma. I couldn't tell them that. So, they were all happy. They believed me when I said I would quit. They thought the matter was over. But it wasn't. Not by a long shot. I owed, I thought, $800, if I turned over the $400 I already had. But Ma had other ideas. She took the money to the clinic down on 14th Street. She said that was the perfect thing to do with "blood" money. There, she said, people "from all walks of life" were treated, and $400 could buy the clinic more supplies. With that, I was back to owing $1,200 to Ripper.

I went out to find Ripper, to talk to him. I wasn't sure what I would tell him, but this thing was getting out of control. I wasn't like the others. Little Tommy's mama didn't know or care what he did. Brad and Taylor were practically alone all the time. Gilly was trying to prove he was a man by making his own stand, no matter what his daddy told him. But I had Grandma and Ma to worry about. I didn't like disappointing them, and besides, after reading that stuff about Martin Luther King and Malcolm X, I knew it was wrong. I knew what Ma had said was right. I had to get out.

Ripper found me first.

"Meeting, tomorrow night," he told me.

I told him that I knew no one was ever supposed to "quit" a gang, especially his, but I had to. I told him my Ma knew about me hanging with him and that I just couldn't do it anymore. He waited patiently while I talked.

"You owe this," he said. "The meeting." No smile. No buddy-buddy routine.

"I owe you money," I said.

"Same thing. You owe me."

I backed off a little. His look was menacing.

"Then we're even," I tried. He laughed at this.

"And 12 big ones." I nodded and walked away, hoping he didn't see that I was shaking.

I was about halfway home when I heard Taylor calling after me. For a second it sounded like old times. It was like he was trying to catch up with me so we could walk together, but that wasn't what he wanted. When he caught up to me, he stopped and bent over for a second to catch his breath.

"So, it's just like that? You just gonna quit like that? Man, I told everyone you were cool. I gave my word that you were cool," he was waving his hands around while he talked.

"Taylor, it's nothing personal, I just can't hang with Ripper anymore. He's bad news, and you know it."

"Yeah? According to who? Your ma? You mama's boy. You have to tell your mama everything you do? You don't see me tellin' mine everything."

I thought about that for a second. He was right; he never told his mother anything, and their relationship stunk. She didn't care what her sons did, and they didn't care what she did. They never talked about anything. I should have said that to him, but I didn't.

"I don't *have* to tell her anything," I shrugged my shoulders. "I tell her what I want to. She asked me about Ripper and the money, and I told her." I started to walk home again. Taylor followed alongside of me.

"You told her about the money? You crazy? Man, you broke the code. I can't believe you. You broke the code!"

"What code?" I stopped and turned to him.

"The code!" He was waving his arms again like a madman. "The code of silence that you swore to take when you joined the Jags. Remember?"

"Yeah, well, I won't be a member of the Jags anymore, not after tomorrow night, so it doesn't really matter, does it?

"What about me?" he asked me.

"What about you?" I didn't know what all this had to do with him.

"I told Ripper you were cool, and now you're makin' me out a fool. Man, think of it, I used to hang out with a guy who tells his mama everything he does." He tried one of Ripper's fake smiles on me and shook his head.

"*Used* to hang out with?" That really made me mad. "Yeah? And what about me, Taylor? I used to have a best friend who got hooked up into a gang and worships the ground Ripper walks on. You can't even think for yourself. You're just like your brother. He jumps around and does everything Ripper tells him to like a puppet. You think you're cool 'cause you can take orders from someone all the time? You're a fool. Don't you know that when you get busted, Ripper isn't gonna help you out? The only reason he pretends to care about you is 'cause he needs an errand boy."

I rolled my eyes at him and walked off. I left him standing there with his mouth kind of hanging open. When I was half a block away from him, he started yelling at me.

"You're the fool! You can't break the code and get away with it. You can't just walk away!"

I just kept on walking. I was proud of the fact that my ma is so cool. I liked the fact that I can tell her just about anything and she will understand. I have a good relationship with her and my grandmother, and that made me feel good. The only reason Taylor made fun of it was because his was so bad. I should have felt sorry for him, but I was still mad.

"You wait and see!" He kept screaming after me. I kept on walking. I had really hoped that things would get back to the way they were before Ripper. I had hoped.

TEN

IT was pouring down rain when Ma stepped off the bus. It was a little after midnight, and she was coming home. She had had to work late. Sometimes that happens. At her night job, it isn't unusual for someone to quit without any notice, and Ma gets stuck cleaning up. She's always the last one out the door at work; she's a good worker.

She got off the bus and opened her umbrella—the one I gave her last Christmas. It was one of the real big ones so that even if there was a wind, the rain wouldn't get on her. The umbrella covered all of her. Maybe that's the reason she didn't see them coming.

She had the umbrella pulled down low over her shoulders to protect her against the rain, so all she could see were her feet. She was hurrying home. It was chilly, and she had her paycheck. Ma told me that it always makes her nervous to come home so late, but when she has her paycheck with her, she is even more worried. She works with a woman who had been mugged, and the guy stole her paycheck. Somehow, he found a way to get it cashed before she called it in.

She was staring down at her feet when she heard other footsteps coming up behind her. She picked up her pace a little and hoped that she would make it to Mr. Phillips' store just around the corner. Once she made it there, she could slip inside and wait for the owners of the footsteps to go away.

She held her purse close to her side and walked on. The sounds got closer and closer. She listened hard for a moment and realized that there were several pairs of feet and they were running. She tilted her umbrella back a little so that she could see better, but when she did, she was face-to-face with Ripper. She gasped and he smiled. She wondered how he had gotten in front of her so quickly. He smiled a slow and scary smile. He knew he scared her.

Suddenly, she realized that she was surrounded by several other teenagers. She looked about her nervously and tried to walk around them, but they moved over and blocked her path. Ripper spoke to her, but the sounds of the rain hitting her umbrella were so loud she couldn't understand him. She just stood there and stared at him, and his smile began to fade.

Rain was dripping off his face, but he didn't even seem to notice that it was raining. He had something else on his mind. He looked around at the other boys and then stretched out his hand as if to ask for her purse. She clutched it even more tightly and shook her head. They both knew what was in the bag. He nodded his head, and one of the boys started to move toward her. He had some kind of lead pipe in his hand.

Ma opened her mouth to scream, but a hand flew over it, and she couldn't make a sound. All anyone could hear were the sounds of the heavy rain hitting the concrete. They dragged her behind the store and began hitting her. They wanted the purse, but no matter how hard they hit her, she wouldn't let go of the bag. She clung on, screaming, but there were no sounds to be heard. Finally, she fell to the ground. Her umbrella caught the wind and blew away.

She lay there bleeding, and the rain was soaking her. Her eyes were wide as she watched the teenagers tear through her bag. They threw things out of it that meant nothing to them. A picture of Grandma and me fell beside her, and she reached out to grab it. Ripper stepped on her hand and smiled down at her. He was laughing.

It was all my fault. If I hadn't quit, she would still be protected. Ripper would have never hurt her, but now he was trying to teach me a lesson. No one ever quit Ripper's gang. No one. And now he was going to make Ma pay. He was going to steal her money and hurt her.

I gasped and sat up with a start. I blinked and looked around the room. It had been a dream. I looked at the clock. It was almost 1 a.m. I slid out of bed and out into the hallway. I could hear the television on and knew that Grandma had fallen asleep in front of it. That meant Ma wasn't home yet. I went into the TV room to wake her up, but she was awake.

"What are you doing up?" we both asked each other. It really was raining outside. I guess I must have heard the thunder in my sleep. I told Grandma about my dream, and she tried to smile and tell me that wasn't going to happen. She put an arm around me and gave me a hug.

We went into the kitchen, and she made me some warm milk. I think it works better on her than me, but she likes to think it makes me go right to sleep, so I drank it down. She told me that even though I had been foolish to think that it was okay to work for Ripper, she and Ma were real proud of me. They knew that I was growing up and I was ready to start making adult decisions.

Pop!

We smiled at each other. The stove thought so too. With the rain falling so heavily, the stove made the kitchen nice and warm.

"You're growing up, and now you've got to learn to make decisions that are good for you and your family," Grandma said. She smiled at me and gave me a kiss. "I know that when the time comes, you'll always make the right decision." I wanted to tell her about the money, but I couldn't. I wanted to tell how deep I was in, but she had said she was proud of me. How proud would she be when she saw how involved I was with Ripper? How could she be proud of me for getting, having, and losing $1,200 in drug money?

We heard a noise at the front door. Ma was home. She knocked some of the rain off the umbrella and stepped inside. When she took off her coat, I noticed that she was wearing the same thing as in my dream. It made me feel a little spooked. She looked startled when she saw that I was waiting for her.

"What are you still doing up?"

"I couldn't sleep. How come you're home so late?"

"Oh, you know how it is. No one wants to be the one to clean up," she said, shrugging her shoulders and giving me a tired smile. She eyed the warm milk and smiled at Grandma. "Mmmm, I'll take some of that if there is any left over."

"You put your worried son to bed, and I'll make you some." Grandma turned and went into the kitchen.

"I don't know what I'd do without you, Mama," Ma laughed as we headed toward my room. When I climbed into bed, she started to fix my covers.

"Ma." I pretended to be annoyed because I'm too old for her to do that, but the truth is, I liked it.

"What?" she asked. "I'll have you know that I kiss you good night every night. You're asleep, but I still tuck you in and kiss you."

I watched her for a second and thought about how much I love her.

"Ma," I said, "I'm sorry if I made you mad."

"No, you never made me mad. It scared me. It scared me to think that someone like Ripper could get so close to you. But I was never mad at you. You are a smart boy, and you have a good head on your shoulders. You will make me proud, I know. You'll do right."

"I told Ripper today that I was out," I said. Her eyes lit up.

"And? What did Mr. Ripper have to say?"

"He didn't like it."

"Hmmm, I bet he didn't. I know how he operates. He doesn't like to lose his pigeons." She sort of nodded at me.

"The thing is, Ma, it's hard, you know? It's hard to break it off because . . ."

Grandma called out that her milk was done. Ma's eyes got big, and she grinned.

"Now, you listen, you just stick to your guns. I'll have a talk with him myself."

"No, don't do that, Ma!" I practically leaped out of bed. "I'll handle it myself."

Grandma called again, anxious to talk about her day of stories.

Pop!

Ma groaned. "You do the right thing, honey." She winked at me and scooted off the bed.

I nodded and rolled over. I never told her about the dream, and I knew Grandma wouldn't either. Why worry her? I fell asleep thinking about Ripper and the way he talked about Ma. The warm milk helped, but it was still hard to sleep.

✻ ✻ ✻

Even Taylor had stopped yelling. Everyone got real quiet. The kid wasn't screaming anymore. From where I stood, I could see that his bare feet were perfectly still. There was no sign of life. Jackson and Brad stepped away from the kid, and I could see all the blood. Gilly was staring at Ripper, waiting for him to say what to do, and Taylor sort of fell off his step trying to see better. When he stumbled, it was the first sound to break the silence.

Ripper looked around to see that it was Taylor and quietly turned back and mumbled something to Gilly. Gilly nodded and looked around. I could see that it hit them that other people might be watching. Gilly nodded to Brad, and the two of them lifted up the kid and began to carry him away. Just like that, I thought. Ripper was so cool. He acted as if nothing had happened. He said something to Jackson and handed him something. Jackson hurried over to the Jones sisters. I was trying to watch to see if he was going to try to bribe them or something, but Ripper blocked my view. I was as tall as he was when I was standing on the second stair. Ripper smoothed his clothes over and tried to steady his voice. He was still panting a little, and I could tell that he did not want to seem out of control. When he caught his breath, he looked at Taylor.

"Why don't you help out and pick up that stuff," he pointed over his shoulder to the shoes

and jacket that had been torn from the kid. "Take it to the pipe . . . no, follow your brother. Give 'em to him." When he said that, I thought about the kid again and looked around, but Brad and Gilly had slipped from sight. It was as simple as that. As fast as the kid came into the neighborhood, he went out.

I realized that Ripper could see that I was looking for the body. Our eyes met.

"Hey, schoolboy," he nodded to me and tried to smile. "I'm not giving up on you just 'cause you gave up on us." He was talking about the Jags. "I know that you still belong and you wouldn't break the code. You know what I'm talkin' about?"

I knew. I knew that for the first time since I'd known Ripper, he was scared. He could pay off the Jones sisters, and he could make sure that all the Jags kept their mouths shut, but he wasn't so sure about me. I had broken the code once. He was afraid I would do it again.

"I like you. You're strong. Not like the others. You can think for yourself. You're smart. At least, that's what I'm countin' on."

I looked up at him and studied his face. He was being sincere. No fake smiles. No fake talk. He was being real. He knew I saw that too. He nodded his head as if to say, "That's right, I'm serious now."

"You play it smart and keep your mouth shut, and no one ever has to get hurt. But if you talk, if you repeat what happened to anyone today, you gonna be an orphan. You got me?" He leaned in real close to my face.

He was so close in my face, I wanted to slug him. He was right there. I felt like I was going to explode. He knew it too. He knew that my one weak spot was my mama and grandma. He knew it.

Just then I heard a noise behind me. It was Grandma.

"What on earth you kids doin' out here?" She looked around to see what had been going on, but the street was deserted. She looked at Ripper for a moment, and then me.

Ripper stared at me to see what I was going to say. I stared back at him.

"Nothing, Grandma. Nothing." I stared into Ripper's eyes while I answered Grandma.

"That was the loudest nothin' I ever heard. I could hardly hear my stories," she shook her head and looked around again before she turned to go in. But Ripper called out to her before she went inside again.

"That's a pretty dress you're wearin', Mrs. Williams. I've seen you wear that on your way to church before."

"Well, thank you." She gave a little smile and disappeared.

I looked back at Ripper, and he was grinning at me. We both knew what that was for. He wanted me to know that he knew when and where my ma and grandma walked.

"I've been meaning to talk to you about that," he shook his head like he was really concerned. "You should talk to your grandma about walking alone to church functions. Especially if it's getting dark outside. She's a small lady. It would be real easy for someone to knock her down, you know?"

That was it! I snapped. I started to come down the stairs at him, but he backed up real fast and laughed. He put his hands up in the air like I was arresting him, and he laughed at me.

"Whoa! Relax. I'm just sayin' it like it is."

By this time, Jackson had come back from talking to the Jones sisters. He was standing beside Ripper. He was laughing too.

He didn't know why he was laughing; he was just doing it because Ripper was.

"You see that? Mike Tyson over here wants to take me on." He elbowed Jackson, and they both laughed some more. Ripper took another step back and stared at my house for a long while, like he was studying it or something.

Then he took a deep breath and pointed a finger at me.

"You just stay smart." And he and Jackson walked away.

ELEVEN

ALL he told us was we were moving into a new area. He didn't tell us that we were going to be in the T-Posse territory. He explained it to us like this: over on 16th Street, near the T area, the new housing development was going up. They had been working on it forever but had begun moving families in last week. Two new markets opened up in the neighborhood too. Everything was new, and I bet the people were really excited about starting over, starting somewhere where their stoves didn't pop.

Ripper was excited too. So far, it was unclaimed territory. Technically, it was on the T-Posse turf, but this was a new section. Ripper saw it as an opportunity to recruit new guys and a new gang. He wanted to start several gangs. He wanted to franchise them, like a string of restaurants or something. Eventually, Gilly would be the leader of the Jags, and Ripper would create a new gang on 16th and appoint a leader there. But he would be the leader of all the leaders. He would be like the president, and we would all be like his senators and congressmen. Ripper was a capitalist with a capital *C*!

"We gonna fight?" Little Tommy asked. Anyone who didn't know Little Tommy would have thought he was chicken, that he was afraid to fight on account of being so little. That wasn't it.

Little Tommy wanted to fight. He liked it. I wasn't so sure how good he really was at it. I mean, if he came across someone bigger, he could get creamed. But Ripper said no fighting. All he wanted was for a large group of us to show up at one of the markets to show how many there were of us.

Ripper had picked the one market on the corner of 16th and S because it was owned by a Korean.

"We gotta let these Gooks know where they stand. He may own the building," Ripper said loudly, "but we own the streets!"

"Yeah!" everyone whooped together.

"We'll trash the place. Send a message once and for all—no Gooks!"

Gook.

Nigger. Chink. Spick. All those words melted together.

We were going into a different neighborhood, into a man's store, and trashing his place because he was new—different. It was like Taylor and me going to Harriet E. Wilson. I was looking to Taylor for help, hoping he would be thinking the same thing. If he was, he didn't show it. He stood next to Brad, while his big brother made all kinds of obscene gestures. He was going to have fun.

Someone said something about the owner having a gun. Ripper laughed and shrugged it off.

"If he gives us any heat," he said, and he patted his stomach under his shirt. Ripper was packing. I wasn't surprised, but I wondered who else was.

There were 11 of us in all. Gilly led the way. Ripper wasn't stupid. He let someone else be the lead man going into the T-Posse turf, while he hung back talking to me. To Gilly, Ripper was just keeping one of his men in line. I knew better. Ripper was letting Gilly be the front man in case of any trouble.

We walked down 14th to S and headed north toward 16th. If there were any Posse members around, they would spot us for sure, and I couldn't help but think that was part of the plan. It was 6:00 in the evening. It was light outside and very busy. People were returning home from work and school. The streets were packed. The market would be busy, and everyone would be out on their stoops watching the world go by. The Jags paraded past everyone like we were right where we were supposed to be.

When we crossed over 16th, I noticed a stirring behind us. While Ripper talked cooly to me about Martin Luther King like he was real interested, I kept a sharp eye out. I counted as many as 30 guys all between the ages of 12 and 20. Most stood around or sat on front stoops, shooting the breeze. Every single one took notice of us. Some got up and followed a little bit. Some fell away, maybe to go report to someone else, but now there was a following of about 10. They hung back, by 30 feet or so, on either side of the street. Like us, they tried to play it cool like it was no big thing. But they were curious.

We saw the store at the corner of S and 16th. It rounded the corner so that it was actually on both 16th and S Streets. It was a good-sized store, the same size as Mr. Phillips'. But Phillips' store has iron-grid screens on the windows and a heavy iron gate that is secured over the front door when the store is closed. He has huge spotlights connected around his building. Like everything else on U, the building with Mr. Phillips' store looks worn and beaten. But this store looked new. You could tell the building was old, but everything was freshly painted. The new owner had put up posters. There were beer, cigarette, and Keebler's cookies posters in the window. The owner even sold Lottery tickets. Suddenly I wished we had this store instead of Phillips'.

When we got to the corner, Gilly slowed so Ripper could push his way forward. He wanted to be the first to walk into the store. One after the other, we all piled in. Immediately, the store owner took notice. There were three people behind the counter—all Korean. A man, a woman (I figured they were the owners), and a boy, about 15 years old, probably their son. Each of them watched us suspiciously as we walked in. Finally, the man said, "Hello," and asked if he could help us with something. I looked out the front window.

Across the street was the group of guys. Some of them stood openly staring at the store—waiting. There was one guy who caught my attention, though. He was about 18 years old. Big. Strong-looking. He leaned against a telephone pole, nonchalantly inspecting his fingernails. He was real cool. Periodically he glanced up at the store but acted like it was of very little interest to him. Anytime anyone asked a question, it was always directed toward him. He would answer without raising his head. Real cool.

Suddenly, there was yelling from the front of the store. I saw Ripper step back, holding his hands up.

"Hey, I'm just telling it like it is." He gave a mocking laugh.

The owner was very angry. "We don't need you here. You go!" He was waving his hand at all of us to leave the store.

Gilly laughed and began imitating the man's accent. His Korean accent was thick, and soon everyone joined in.

Ripper waved a finger tauntingly at the owner. "You'll be sorry," he said.

While all this went on, Little Tommy and Taylor loaded up with goods. Candy bars, potato chips, colas. Everything they could stuff into their clothes, they did. Others joined in. While the store owner was yelling at Ripper and Gilly, he looked over Ripper's shoulder and saw Little Tommy.

"You. You stop. I call police."

As we all hurried out of the store, I saw Ripper out of the corner of my eye. He whipped out his piece and held it sideways in the face of the boy. The boy and his parents were frozen. I could hear the mother crying. The father wasn't yelling anymore. He was talking very calmly. He was trying to talk Ripper down. I couldn't hear what Ripper was saying, and Little Tommy was pushing against my back to get out of the store, him and all his goods. Whatever Ripper said, it was definitely a threat.

Everyone followed Gilly in a half-walk, half-run. It was important to look cool but get the hell out of there.

We turned right onto 15th, headed back to U, but Ripper pulled back. He still had some unfinished business. At 15th, he turned left and headed for the intersection of 15th and T. He was looking for the Posse. Even Gilly was uncomfortable with this. It was one thing to come one-on-one with a gang on no-man's-land, but doing it on the gang's own turf was bad news.

There was a break between the row houses like a little alley. No cars sat there, just piles of trash. Mostly, I saw paint spray cans. I knew they were the poor man's high. I was staring at the pile of discarded cans, when there it was—a foot. Poking out from behind the side of a shed and trash. Then another and another. They stepped out in force. There was no big announcement, no sign or colors, but it was as clear as day: this was the T-Posse. No question, they had been waiting for us. It was instantaneous. Everyone saw everyone at once. No one spoke. Not a word. The Jags stopped in midstep. The T-Posse stepped out into the alleyway. All that was heard was the sound of sneakers dragging on the pavement and little rocks and pebbles being carelessly kicked to the side, while each man stepped in beside another so that at last, the Jags and T-Posse were faced off.

The man I had tagged as the Posse leader had aligned himself with Gilly. Ripper's plan had worked somewhat. They definitely thought Gilly was the lead man. Ripper was lined up across from some other tough-looking dude—big and mean-looking, smiling like he was welcoming home long-lost relatives. Across from me was a 15- or 16-year-old looking kid—tall, skinny. I scanned him. He was packing. His shirt rumpled on his right hip. He had done a sloppy job of pulling his shirt over, or maybe he was rushed. I quickly looked the group over. Most looked as my guy did—hurried, but ready. I was sure each had his own heater. I was bare. And I knew Taylor was clean too. My heart was pounding so loudly, it was hard to think. It was hard to pay attention to details. I was thinking about home, Ma, my school assignment, and my stinking, loser father for leaving us alone.

The Posse leader stepped forward. No one else moved. His eyes practically burned holes into Gilly. Gilly didn't move. He was unsure of what to do. Did he look away—break eye contact and look the coward? Did he call out Ripper's name? Why wasn't Ripper saying anything? Gilly had played the tough man but found himself in a spotlight he wasn't sure he was ready for.

The T-Posse sensed all this. Some shifted, some chuckled low under their breath. Gilly looked scared.

"Can I help you?" the leader finally asked mockingly. It was an in-your-face tone.

"Naw, man, we're okay," Gilly squeaked out. Ripper shifted a little, moving closer to Gilly, and Ripper's Posse man moved with him. The T-Posse was definitely coached on how to stare down their men. My man never took his eyes off me. Even while Gilly and their leader talked, my man burned holes in my skull.

"Now, I know," and he exaggerated the words as sarcastically as he could, "you wasn't steppin' into my hood just to go grocery shoppin'." More chuckles. More shifting of the feet. I let my eyes fall back on my man. I stared back at him. *He was going to kill me.* No matter what I did—run, fight—all he had to do was pull out his piece, and I was a dead man.

"Heard the new store sold licorice sticks," Ripper stepped forward. "I'm just crazy for 'em." The Posse leader never moved his body. He stayed perfectly still except his eyes moved over to the right. He looked Ripper up and down. As bad as things had been, as much as Ripper had made me sick to my stomach, he made me glad I was on his side. He was so cool, so confident. He offered the guy a licorice stick. He *actually* had one.

"I don't think I was talkin' to you," the other guy growled.

"I think you was." Ripper's voice was flat, deep, powerful.

It was something everyone sensed. *This* was the man the Posse leader wanted to be talking to, or maybe not.

There was some silence. While my man continued to stare at me, I watched the leader. I was thinking about Ripper. Thinking about what to say or to do. The Posse leader knew one thing—Ripper was not a guy to mess with. Ripper spoke again, but there was no play in his voice this time. He took away the candy.

"You got some kind of claim to that store?" It wasn't a question really. It was a challenge.

"You Ripper?" the other guy spoke.

"You got that right."

"So I meet the famous Ripper," he broke out into a smile. Confident. Equally dangerous. "I'm T. J."

"I don't care," Ripper shot back. There had been a slight smile on T. J.'s face, like he was hot stuff, but it quickly faded when Ripper said this. It made T. J. mad, embarrassed him. Ripper was supposed to have heard of T. J. too. Ripper was supposed to say something back to acknowledge T. J.

T. J. eyed Gilly for a second and moved over so that he stood toe-to-toe with Ripper.

"I think you forgot where you was, Ripper," T. J. said. He was so close to Ripper's face, he was breathing all over him. Ripper never flinched.

I had been watching, and yet, I never saw it happen. It was all a blur. I vaguely saw Ripper moving, catlike. He took a giant step back, his right shoulder dropped down, and then, *bam!* Ripper was back in T. J.'s face with a gun pressed against his cheekbone, under his left eye. Ripper held it gangsta-style, gun sideways, hand over top. His pinky stuck straight out, his index finger on the trigger.

Several people jumped, guns out, same position, readied. My heart was pounding now harder than ever. This was it! There were too many guys holding too many guns for someone not to get trigger-happy. T. J.'s right-hand man had moved as quickly as Ripper, only he held his gun against Ripper's left temple. Gilly stood between Ripper and the right-hand man, gun cocked, pressing it against right-hand man's forehead. No one moved. No one spoke. Guns were everywhere. For the first time, I looked away from the pileup of guns between Ripper and T. J. and looked at my man. He held a gun leveled straight at me.

The gun was menacing; the face wasn't. For the first time, I saw through the stare-down. The kid didn't look happy about this. He held the gun, but he was as scared as me. He had probably been handed the gun just before they set out to find us. He looked uncomfortable. He held it hand over, steadied right on my face, but it didn't look natural. I could tell he felt awkward, didn't like holding a gun on a kid—even younger than him.

Everyone else it seemed was carrying. Little Tommy, Brad, Jackson, Kewee, and Joey all had guns drawn. Every one of the Posse held a piece. Only Taylor and me stood alone, unprotected. Right then I was wishing I had a gun.

Then three things happened at the same time. It's funny. We stood there for so long with nothing happening, no one saying a word. No one moved, talked, or shot, much less blinked. Then, just like that, everything went crazy. Ripper had opened his mouth to say something. Knowing him, it was going to be a dare or a threat. He was probably just waiting for a reason to shoot the guy's brains out. Just when he opened his mouth, a siren cried out, only more like half a siren, one of those where the cops just want you to know they see you.

As Ripper started to talk and the siren gave us a start, someone fired a shot. I don't know who; I just know that it turned into the Wild West. I dove sideways, rolled against the side of the shed, and dove into a pile of spray cans. I don't think my man ever shot at me. I smashed into the trash pretty hard and rolled over to look where I was, to see if any gun was on me. There he was—standing still, staring. He watched me for half a second, glanced up to the police cruiser coming down the alley, and turned. He took off like a rocket and disappeared between two row houses. That was it. That was the last I ever saw of him.

I turned back and saw the nose of the cruiser making its way past the shed. The car jerked to a halt, and I knew the cops were getting out. I shoved away at the trash, jumped to my feet, and took after the kid with the gun. I didn't want him; I just wanted out.

It's amazing how much your brain can process in a couple of seconds, you know? Right when I was turning over, to get to my feet and run, I looked over to the side. Little Tommy was standing there. It's all I can remember. He had his gun out, but I couldn't quite make out what he was doing. He was looking toward the ground. Ripper was down! He was half-sitting, holding his side, blood everywhere. He looked like he was in a lot of pain, unable to move, maybe in shock. Gilly was squatted down beside him, gun held out, hand over, leveled at someone, and he was firing. Cops are right there, and he's squeezing off the trigger!

I bolted out of there, running as fast as I could. I was nearly hit by a car crossing over 14th, but I never stopped. I heard tires squealing, two or three cars honking at me, but I streaked across the busy street, turned up U, and headed straight home, never once looking back.

U never looked so good to me. Familiar faces. The Jones sisters were outside with some of the other neighborhood girls, jumping rope. Mrs. Clovis was outside with a grocery cart, looking up at the second floor talking to Ms. Walker, who was partially hanging out her window. Ms. Walker's boy was working on one of his cars. He worked in some auto shop and was always dragging home cars to repair and sell. Some of the guys hung around his car, laughing and joking while he worked under the hood. There were a few more people up the street coming home from work.

As I ran passed Jeff Walker and his buddies, I saw him pull his head back from the car a little and give me a worried look. The girls skipping rope gave me a look, and one of them said something to the others, but no one said anything to me. I ran up the front steps to the second floor and through my front door. Grandma was in the kitchen, so I knew I was safe. I hollered "hi!" Then I slammed my door and fell back onto my bed. Staring up at the ceiling, I tried to catch my breath and take in what had just happened. I remembered everything, every detail, because it played in slow motion in my mind, over and over and over again.

If I thought I could escape what had happened, I was way off. It wasn't a matter of acting cool and hoping Ma and Grandma wouldn't catch on to something happening. The grapevine hit their ears long before anything else. Everyone in the hood would soon know what went down on 15th and S. The leader of the T-Posse had pulled a gun on Ripper when they were squared off and shot him in the side, just missing his gut. Gilly was arrested for assault. He shot a kid from the Posse. Both Ripper and the kid were in the hospital. Brad was shot, grazed in the shoulder. Taylor never left his side, and the two were taken into custody but released. Neither one had a gun. I wasn't sure how that could be since I saw Brad with a piece myself, but I figured Taylor dumped it for him before the cops took them. Little Tommy was spending the night in juvenile detention—possession of an illegal firearm. It sounded like only three or four of us made it out of there. I learned all this later.

I holed up in my room all night, telling Grandma I was doing homework, and held her off that way. Who knew if the grapevine had already reached her? I thought I'd play it cool, wait it out and see what happened the next day. Grandma had other ideas. She called Ma at work, and Ma hopped on the next bus. Ma never took off work, so I was really surprised when I saw her.

I sneaked out to the bathroom to take a shower while Grandma was watching shows. When I came back into my room, towel clutched around my waist, I nearly dropped it when I saw Ma sitting on my bed.

"Ma!" I stopped at the doorway. She was sitting casually on my bed, in the middle of my dirty clothes, basketball, shoes, comic books, and junk. She didn't say a word about any of it. In fact, she acted like she didn't even notice.

"I need to talk to you," she said.

I was standing there soaking wet, wearing nothing but a towel. I shifted. "Well . . ." I looked down at myself to let her see that I was naked.

"You can get dressed," she shrugged. My mouth fell open.

"Ma, I can't get dressed with you sitting there."

"I won't look." She turned and faced the little dresser I had beside my bed. Sitting on top of it was an alarm clock and the journal. I had been looking at it before I decided that I stunk and needed to take a shower. She reached over and picked it up.

"Don't!" I started. She turned and looked at me. "I mean, just sit there. I'll be right back." I grabbed my underwear, some shorts, and a shirt from the top of the dresser and ran back into the bathroom. Those were the only clean clothes I had in the room. If it was on the dresser top, it was clean. Grandma put the clean stuff there. For principle, she said she wouldn't put my stuff away for me, that I should learn to do that for myself. So mostly, the clothes stayed on top of my dresser. I didn't do it on purpose. I just never got around to putting things away. Now I wished I had, especially my journal.

My mind was racing. Why was she home from work, wanting to talk to me? Grandma went to her bedroom. Usually that meant that it was going to be serious. Whenever there was something really serious, Grandma thought it should be a mother/son thing and disappeared. I jumped around on the wet bathroom floor, trying to poke my feet through the underwear holes, knowing that Ma was thumbing through my journal. If I didn't hurry, she'd read the whole thing. After smashing twice into the sink, I made it back into my room. Ma was just sitting there. No journal. I sighed.

"Grandma called me at work. She heard . . ." and Ma filled me in on what she knew about what had gone down with the T-Posse. My mouth just hung open. I hadn't known any of it. I figured they had all made it out like me. I figured everyone had bolted like me. She studied my face for a moment.

"Were you there?"

"What?" I was stalling. Man, was I stalling, but I couldn't think of anything. It was so stupid, you know? I should have just confessed right up front. But the only thing I could think to do was deny it.

"No, Ma," I said. My voice kind of whined.

"You weren't?" she asked.

"Naw. I wasn't there. I was, you know, hangin' out. I wasn't there, Ma."

"You weren't there?" she repeated. I was beginning to get uneasy. She knew something. She was feeling me out.

"No."

"I hear otherwise." She was testing me. We stared at each other for a couple of minutes.

"What?"

"I heard you were there." There was an edge to her voice. I didn't see this side of her very much. Mostly, I'm good. I don't give her any hassles. We all get along fine. It isn't Ma's way to be mean or tough. But she can be. You'd better believe she can.

"It wasn't me, Ma," I said again. I made sure my eyes were wide, that I looked as sincere as possible. I was in it this far; there was no turning back now. Besides, I thought about it, and there was no way any of those guys would name who was there. The only reason anyone knew something went down was because Brad and Ripper got shot. Little Tommy and some others were busted. That was the only reason.

"Because, you know, it would break my heart if I knew you were there. You know that?" she said. I nodded.

All of a sudden she reached over and picked up my Malcolm X book and studied it.

Malcolm X had one of those faces that the more you look at it, the more you like it. He had a good face.

"What do you want to do?" Ma asked suddenly. She looked up from the book and studied me.

"Huh?"

"With your life, boy? What do you want to do?"

"Aw, Ma," I said, stepped forward, and reached for the book. The last thing I wanted was to get into one of those conversations. But she pulled the book back, out of my reach.

"I mean it." She was serious. I stood back.

I shrugged. It was the only thing I could think of to do. I didn't like Ma this way. In ways, she was scarier than Ripper.

"You got goals? You got things you want to see happen, like an education? Nice home, car?" She was counting off on her fingers.

"Ma," I laughed. "You know I do. That's why I'm going to Harriet E. Wilson. I'm going to make things better for all of us, like you always say."

"Hmmm." She nodded to herself. "You know, baby, life is hard."

I moaned.

"Now I mean it, you listen up." Her voice rose a little, and I straightened up. "It's hard. Right when things seem to be going good, something else tries to knock you down. Not 'cause you're black or from this neighborhood, just 'cause. Life is like that. But bein' black and poor doesn't make it any easier. You've got to work harder, be better, just to break even." She looked down at my book and tapped the cover, right over Malcolm's face.

"He could tell you that. Twice as hard, twice as good. That'll get you where you need to go." She was talking more to herself than to me. But suddenly, she looked straight back at me. "So, why do you want to go and make things harder? Huh, boy? You hang out with gangs, with Ripper, around drugs and bad kids. It'll tear you down. The best of men have fallen."

"I know that, Mama," I said quietly.

"No, I don't think you do. I think you think you're playing a game." Her voice was changing. Her tone was changing. She got up off the bed and began to pace around the room, causing me to shrink back along the wall and eventually sit down on my bed by the pillow.

She stopped and studied the book cover for what seemed like a very long time. She spoke. Not to me. Not to the book. Just out loud, her voice rising like she was giving a sermon. The passion in her voice was real. She wasn't angry, and she sounded sort of scared.

"*You* have to believe that you can make things better. *You* have to believe that you can make things happen. *You* have to believe that all things are possible. And then *you* have to make it happen. No one but you can make it happen. You have to tell yourself that you have a plan, that you have a purpose and a mission, and *you* have to follow the path that'll take you where you need to be. You have to ask yourself all the time, 'Is this going to take me to the right path? Is this going to take me where I need to be?' "

We stared at each other for a while. I was the first to break away. I stared down at my pillow. She didn't move. I guessed she was waiting for some kind of response.

"I got a plan," I said meekly.

"I want to hear it," she said.

Oh. I thought for a minute. I'd never really thought about an actual plan before. Geez, I was only 13 years old. I didn't think about things like life plans.

"I'm, uh, going to finish school with good grades and get a scholarship to Howard University. Probably writing," I said, suddenly seeing my journal. "I like to write," I told her. "I'm good at it." I always got good marks in writing, and it was different from the other subjects. They were like assignments, but writing was real. It felt good, like I was supposed to be doing it.

Ma folded her arms, head cocked to the side, waiting.

"If I go to Howard, I could stay close to home. I could always be here for you and Grandma, but I'll live at Howard with my scholarship money. And when I graduate I'll get a good-payin' job, something to take us out of here, maybe get a house in Arlington. You could work one job, but only if you wanted to. We'd be good for money," I told her. A slow smile crept over her face. Her arms dropped to their sides.

"That's it? That's your goal?" I looked at her for a second. I couldn't figure how she meant that. Was she making fun? I nodded after another second.

"Yeah, Ma, that's what I want."

"That's what you *want* or that's your *goal*?" she pushed me. I rolled my eyes a little.

"It's my goal."

She stepped forward and gave me a kiss on the top of my head. "That sounds like a fine goal to me, baby." She turned and headed out, but as she got to the doorway with her hand on the doorknob, she turned back to me and said, "Now you need to ask yourself how you can make your goals happen." She shut the door.

TWELVE

HOWARD University sounded good. I had just made it up, but it all sounded really good. Howard University is in Washington, D.C. I could stay close to Ma, make sure she was okay. I could take care of her when I was older. I knew she had liked that too. I had heard her talking to Grandma about her baby growing up. I knew she worried about things.

I settled back on the bed, put my arms behind my head, and stared up at the ceiling. Arlington had sounded good too. Imagine us moving into one of those big white houses with the perfect yards and rounded bushes that line the sidewalks. We'd have a two-car garage and cars! I lay there and thought about what kind of cars we would have. No more bus trips for Ma.

Pop!

I smiled. Even with my door shut, I could hear the stove. As much as Ma hated it, I might have to take the stove with us when we moved. Maybe I would put it in our basement and buy a new stove for Ma. I should have told her that. Part of my plan was to buy her a new "pop"less stove.

I didn't exactly have it in my head what kind of job I would have, but I would be making good money—double or triple what Ma was making, and that would be working only one job. It would be in Arlington too, and I wondered how our new neighbors would feel about us. Would they call us "niggers"?

The whole thing was screwed up. My mind suddenly changed from the peaceful dream world of Arlington to Ripper. To how everything went down. He had picked a market just because the owners were Korean. It was all so crazy. People had hated Malcolm X because they thought he was a racist, but some people hated him and Martin Luther King just for being black. Ripper threatened a Korean family just for being Korean. I still caught crap sometimes for being black in a mostly white school. I couldn't figure it out.

Ma had told me there was a famous religious leader in the black community. He had actually known Malcolm X and Martin Luther King, but he was different. He was always in the news for making anti-Jewish and anti-Korean remarks. He hated anyone and everyone who wasn't black. Ma said his kind was very dangerous. It was like the thing with Ripper or the politicians. This guy wanted power, and if he could get it through making people afraid of one another, making them angry with others, he would do it. There was always one kind of gang or another, always after power, always taking down the little guy.

I thought about the Latino kid who had come into our neighborhood. That kid was really stupid. Imagine walking into someone else's neighborhood like that. I thought about those new shoes and warm-up outfit he was wearing, and it made me mad. I couldn't believe that a kid could be that stupid. I tried to convince myself that he had that beating coming to him for being so dumb. Blaming him was the only thing I could do that helped get him out of my head and helped to make me feel better about keeping quiet.

The story had been all over the place for a week or so, and local leaders had put up a $10,000 reward for information about his disappearance. Every time something came on about it, Grandma walked around the kitchen clucking her tongue. It hadn't really made the news so much lately. Ripper had told us to stay quiet and it would go away. He was right. Every day there was less and less interest. So why couldn't I get that stupid kid out of my head?

I got out of bed to get something to drink but stopped when I opened the door and heard Ma's voice. She and Grandma were talking in the kitchen.

"You think he was there?" Grandma asked. Ma sighed heavily. I bit my lip.

"I just got this feeling. He was there," she said. I stared down at the floor. I should have told her but couldn't. She was just better off not knowing, and yet, she did anyway.

"You tell him that?" Grandma asked. I could hear her patting Ma's leg or something. I could see it in my mind. Grandma and Ma are like that. They're real close, always hugging or patting each other. Grandma felt real bad that Ma had to work so hard.

"I tried telling him I knew he was there, but he just denied it. What am I gonna do, Mama?" she asked. There was silence. I leaned out more into the hallway and listened. She was crying. I heard Grandma scoot her chair forward and comfort her baby. I winced. For a second, I was almost mad at Ma. Why does she do this to me? Man, I was feeling bad. And all this started because I was trying to help her out, help us all out. I stepped out and leaned against the wall.

"It's all right, baby," Grandma was saying. Her voice was low, soothing, almost musical, and

I knew she had Ma in a big hug. The kind of hug only mothers know how to give. Ma is the best at it, but it had been a long time since I had needed one of those kinds of hugs. I wouldn't have minded one so much just then.

"He never used to lie about this kind of thing. He never used to be in this kind of thing." Her voice was breaking up, and it gave me a stomachache. I stood helplessly in the hall, listening. "Guns? Those boys had guns. Oh, Mama, he could have been . . . you know how easy it could have been him that was shot?"

"I know it, honey, but it wasn't. He's a good boy; he's got a good head on his shoulders."

Ma was mumbling something. I could tell her face was buried into Grandma's shoulder. She was scared. Not for me now, but that I could have been shot, and I thought about how close I came, really thought about it for the first time. If Ma had seen me lookin' down the barrel of the gun, she'd have died.

"He's everything I got, Mama. If he . . ." She was silent for several minutes. "How can I fight Ripper? I can't offer him that kind of money. How can I fight someone like Ripper dangling all that money in front of my boy's face?"

The house was real quiet for a long time. I could hear small sniffles and knew they were both crying. They were scared. I pushed my head against the wall, face up toward the ceiling, and let the tears fly. I didn't care anymore. It was easier to just let loose.

Pop!

More silence. Then I heard a chair scoot back. Ma was on her feet. She sniffed one final time.

"I'll be damned if I'm gonna let the likes of Ripper take him from me." Her voice had changed. It was loud. It was back to that sermon voice.

"That's the way, baby."

"If he wants to play dirty, he'll have to play it with me," her voice thundered. I knew now she was talking for effect. She wanted me to hear her. She wanted me to hear her through the walls.

My tears stopped. *Oh God, no, Ma.* I was suddenly scared. I didn't want Ma messing with Ripper.

In the next 30 minutes, I had a real, live nightmare. Ma called the neighbors, local pastors of two different churches, and the police to arrange a meeting. She asked Reverend Loe to invite his congregation from T Street and the Korean family from the market to join in the meeting.

By the time I went to bed, it went from an idea to an all-out community war on Ripper, the

Jags, and the T-Posse. They called it "Taking Back Our Streets," invited Channel 5 TV to come out, and arranged for the meeting to take place at the St. Ives Baptist Church.

The next day at school, I tried to talk to Taylor about it, but he wouldn't talk to me. I tried to talk to him about what happened to Brad, everything. We were out on the basketball courts, and Taylor was playing some ball. I kept calling his name, but he just ignored me. The word was already out that Ma was heading up the "Taking Back Our Streets" campaign.

Finally, after he missed an easy shot, he came over to where I was standing and asked me what I wanted. I was trying to talk about yesterday and how sorry I was about Brad and the others. I wanted to talk about the Latino kid. I wanted to talk about everything that had been going down. Taylor looked a little relieved and started to agree with me, but then his face fell. I looked over to see what he saw—Little Tommy Watson standing across the blacktop with his arms folded. He was checking us out. Taylor looked down at the ground and mumbled, "Don't talk to me, man," and walked away.

I looked back at Little Tommy. He stared back at me, and then the bell rang. He turned and walked away like he was so cool. I was starting to see him as he really was. I had been right the first time. He was nothing but a geek trying to be a gangsta.

Everyone went inside except Taylor, Little Tommy, and a few other kids. I saw them standing at the side of the school, out of sight of the teachers. I watched for a second and then went inside. I didn't want to be a part of any of that anymore; I just wanted out, and I wanted to take Taylor with me.

When the second bell rang, there was still no Taylor. He hadn't come back to class, so I figured he had skipped out for the rest of the day. Ms. Whitley even asked me where he was, and I just shrugged my shoulders. She eyed me for a second. I guess she figured I was covering for him, but I really didn't know.

After class, she tried to stop me and ask me what was going on with Taylor. I knew that his grades were falling and he wasn't doing his assignments. He thought he was too cool for that. He was blowing everything off for Ripper. And Ripper was the same guy who was saying how important it was to stay in school. Ripper was a liar. He didn't want Taylor to stay in school. He wanted to make sure that everyone stayed dumb and listened to everything he told them.

I went to my locker and was getting out my books to go home when Amy Boyd came running up to me. She's in my grade and is pretty nice. She's from Arlington. White, blonde, blue eyes. The whole bit. But she isn't the kind who cares if I'm from a different neighborhood. I figured she has a good mama.

"Taylor got beat up behind the school. They beat him up bad." She was talking so fast I could hardly understand her.

"What?"

"Taylor! He got beat up real bad. He's got blood all over him." She was jumping up and down. "You better go help him. He's going home."

I took off running. He had been stupid lately. I hadn't been liking him much, but he was still my best friend, you know? Since we were real little, he'd been there for me. I took the stairs two at a time and ran down the hallway, dodging kids, and out the back door. I could see several adults standing around Taylor. As I got closer, I could see that he was a mess. He was arguing with the adults. I recognized two of them; they were teachers.

"No, I just want to go home," I could hear him yelling. His voice sounded really strained. I think he was about to cry. He jerked his arm away from one of the teachers and started to walk off.

"You need to let the nurse clean you up. You don't want to get an infection, do you?"

That was a stupid question. Adults just don't understand kids. Taylor just got beat up on school grounds, and everyone in the whole school knew about it. The last thing he'd care about was an infection. I wiggled my way through the adults and looked at Taylor.

"Hey," I looked at his face. He had a bloody nose and lip. His lip was getting fatter by the second, and his left eye was beginning to swell shut. He looked awful. He had blood all over the front of his shirt, and his back and pants were covered with grass and dirt. "You look pretty cool," I grinned. I heard one of the teachers gasp. I guess she thought that was the worst thing I could say, like I was all for him fighting.

I knew he felt embarrassed. I could tell that he just wanted to get out of there. The worst thing I could have said was how bad it looked. Taylor tried to laugh a little, but it hurt his face. I put an arm around him, like buddies do, and told the teachers that my grandmother was a nurse. It wasn't really a lie. She could have been if she had wanted to.

The teachers weren't very sure about letting us walk off, but they didn't have a choice; we just started walking. When we got to the edge of the school grounds, I could see the principal running out. Amy Boyd had told him, I bet. We just walked faster and pretended not to hear a thing.

We walked all the way to the bus stop and never said a word. Taylor just hung his head down and hoped that no one would notice him. When we got on the bus, the driver took one look at his face and whistled. Another woman winced and leaned forward to ask if he was okay.

We sat down and Taylor looked at me.

"Is it that bad?" He was really embarrassed.

"Yeah," I made a face at him. "You look kind of tough, though."

"Yeah, right," he said and kicked the seat in front of him.

I stared at his face for a second and remembered that Little Tommy was the last person I saw with Taylor.

"So what happened?"

"Your mama happened," he snapped.

"What?"

"Your mama and this 'Taking Back Our Streets' thing."

"Yeah," I sighed. I knew something bad was going to happen from all this. It was something

Ma just couldn't understand. She didn't understand that she just couldn't challenge Ripper without bad things happening. "But what does that have to do with your face?"

"I was talking to you." He picked up the end of his T-shirt and dabbed at his nose. It was still bleeding a little. "A warning."

My mouth fell open, but he kept talking. His voice lowered. He was more than embarrassed and hurt. He was angry. "But he shouldn't have done this," Taylor muttered. "He'll be sorry."

"How?" I wanted to know. It was as though my voice brought Taylor back to reality, because he jerked his head up like he didn't realize he'd even said anything out loud. He hesitated.

"I got Ripper's gun," he spoke softly.

"What?"

"Yeah, when the cops came in, there was no time. Ripper was on the ground. The dude, T. J., shot him, but Ripper sent off a round before he went down. The guy's laid up in the hospital—Ripper's job. Got him in the back. He's bad off." I continued to stare. "Brad was holdin' too. When he saw the cops, he tossed me his and Ripper's to get rid of them."

Nice. I didn't say it, but I was thinking what a jerk Brad was. He would let Taylor get busted for holding guns before he'd let Ripper or himself. I just listened as Taylor continued to tell how he'd dumped the guns before the cops moved in. By the time he got back, he realized that Brad had been hit too. Brad and Ripper were taken to the hospital, and Taylor went with them. He looked around to make sure no one could hear him.

I looked around too and noticed that we were outside my house. I had been so into what Taylor was saying, I hardly remembered getting off the bus or passing Mr. Phillips'. We started to go inside so that Grandma could clean him up when Taylor groaned.

"I can't believe I got this 'cause of you," he said.

"I don't get that, man," I said, shaking my head. He looked awful. It was hard to believe that Little Tommy, "family," had done this.

"If your mama doesn't lay off the press and everyone, this could happen to her." The words stung.

A thousand years passed by. I stood there on my front stoop and looked at my buddy's swollen, bloodied face. I was paralyzed with fear. I tried to erase the image of my mother looking like that, but it was too late. To show me how serious he was, Ripper had made Taylor a guinea pig.

"Why didn't they just hit me?" I yelled. I was yelling at the top of my lungs. "Why didn't they just beat me up?"

"Gilly says it wouldn't have hurt as much," Taylor's voice was dulled, very calm. Too calm. I fell back on to the step, dazed. Taylor sat next to me, and we stared out into the street.

He was right. This hurt way more. And I thought about how evil Ripper and Gilly really were. Only a real mean sucker could have thought of something like this. Some family. Ripper was always saying how when you belong to the gang, it is like being part of a family. I knew he was worried about me leaving, that I would tell certain things, and now Ma was stirring up trouble, but this . . . I had never expected this sort of thing. And if he would or could do this to Taylor, what would he do to Ma?

"Now do you believe me? Ripper and Gilly don't care 'bout you or anyone else. They just want to make sure everyone does what they say." I knew he knew it. It had to hurt. Taylor really wanted to believe in Ripper. He liked the idea that he was going to be rich and powerful one day. Ripper made him believe all the lies.

"I know," he said. "And he's going to be sorry."

I looked at his swollen face. It looked so bad, he almost looked evil. I knew he was humiliated and mad. "You gonna shoot Ripper?"

That's when it hit me. Insurance.

I must have said it out loud because Taylor said, "What insurance?"

"To protect you and Ma, me, everyone. If Gilly or Ripper tries anything like this again, we can turn the gun over to police, or say we will." At that point, it seemed like a good idea.

❖ ❖ ❖

We were at the very edge of the pipe. Taylor flipped on his flashlight and started inside. He turned around and looked at me. He was only a few steps inside, and already he was a shadow.

"Now, remember, the minute you hear anything, make a noise." Then he turned and walked down the tunnel. When he had walked about ten feet, I couldn't even see him anymore. All I could see was his light bouncing around as he walked.

"I can't really remember where I dropped it," he said loudly, and his voice echoed off the walls. It sounded weird. He had been running so fast when he dropped the gun, it could be anywhere. He was talking to himself. All I could hear were strange echo sounds. I just watched the light bounce around in the tunnel and listened for anyone who might be coming. I could hear Taylor splashing around and knew that he was running his hands through the sewer water searching for the gun. I was thinking how gross that was when I heard a noise above me. It was kind of a scraping noise that rang throughout the pipe. Then I heard Taylor.

"Oh, yeah! I found it, I found it! It's just been lying here!" I could see his light jumping around and knew that he was too. Then the light flipped up toward me. He was running toward me, splashing and yelling. I guess he had been really scared of what Ripper could do. Especially after we saw what he did to that Latino kid and to T. J. I guess Taylor was afraid for his life.

I was just about to yell back at him when I heard another noise. I stepped out for a minute and saw the back of Gilly. He was standing on top of the tunnel. He had turned around and was talking to someone. They were on their way down. I knew that we'd never get out without being seen. If they walked down the side, that would give Taylor and me enough time to run inside and hide. Hiding seemed a lot better than facing Gilly.

I ran inside and shushed Taylor as quietly as I could. When I met his light, I whispered that Gilly and the others were standing above the pipe.

"What?" Taylor whispered frantically. "Oh, man, we're dead."

"No, you got the flashlight. Let's just run all the way down the pipe." I tugged on his shirt, and we started down the pipe.

It was hard to run and not make noises in the water. Taylor aimed the light down at the ground so we could see. When I heard some voices at the end of the tunnel, I grabbed the light from Taylor and flipped off the switch. We slowed down and tried to walk as quietly as possible. We were about a half a block from the entrance. We could see their figures in the mouth of the tunnel. I knew that any minute Gilly was going to turn on his flashlight. We were still close enough to be seen. But suddenly there was some yelling, and we both stopped. It was Brad.

He was the last one to enter the pipe. It was like he had just caught up to the others. I could tell he was still hurting from being shot. His shoulder was heavily bandaged.

"What the hell did you do that for, Gilly?" he yelled, and his voice bounced all the way down to us.

"What? Your brother? Listen, man, that was a mistake. Little Tommy was just taking initiative, but he got the wrong guy. I wanted 'Schoolboy' to get the message, not your brother." He sounded so sincere.

"That's not true." Taylor whispered in my ear. "Little Tommy said the way it was. Gilly's lying."

I hit his arm to make him be quiet and listened. Gilly was the big man now that Ripper was in the hospital. He was explaining that he wasn't so sure I could be trusted and that he just wanted a message to be sent to me. He said that he was sorry that it had to be through Taylor, but maybe it had worked out for the best. Deep down, I know that Taylor was hoping that Brad would fight Gilly for hurting his little brother, but Brad just shrugged his shoulders and agreed with Gilly. Brad was so weak, he couldn't even stand up for his own brother. I felt Taylor let out a little sigh, and I knew that he was crushed. He had always thought Brad was the greatest when he was little. Now he realized his brother was just a big jerk.

While they talked, we continued to creep backwards, hoping that no one would turn on a light. We only had a little bit more to go and the pipe would turn. We would be able to flip on the light again and run to the other end of the tunnel. Taylor felt the edge of the pipe, where it turns, and gave me a poke. We had both just turned around when Gilly flipped on his light. At the far end of the tunnel, they were able to make out two figures.

They couldn't see who we were, but they knew we were there.

"Hey," Gilly shouted, "look there!" He pointed and started running after us. Taylor flipped on his light again, and we began to run with everything we had. Our feet were splashing hard down the narrow pipe. The sounds of the Jags running and yelling behind us helped us run even faster. It echoed through the tunnel and sounded like a freight train was coming. The light was dancing around, making it hard to run. While Taylor ran, the light would go up and down. Sometimes there was total darkness on the floor of the pipe; I couldn't see a thing. I kept getting the feeling that I was going to fall and crack my head open.

We ran for about another block. I could see a light behind us and knew that they were gaining on us, but I could see the end of the tunnel and knew we could make it. I heard Taylor say something, and then I saw it. There were bars on the end of the tunnel. It was like a big grate over the whole mouth of the pipe.

"We can fit. We can fit!" I yelled at Taylor.

I kept running full blast to the bars. I never slowed up until I was on them. I put my hands out to catch myself against the bars and smashed through. The side of my head hit one of the bars hard, but I was able to slide through. Taylor was right behind me, and I could see that the Jags had just turned the corner. Ten more steps, and they would be able to see who we were. Taylor hit the bars and slid through too. He's a little bigger than me, so he really had to squeeze.

As soon as he was through, we both cut to the right of the pipe and began running up the hill that led out to the main street. When we were out of sight and about halfway up the hill, I could hear them hit the bars. They were way too big to squeeze through. Only Little Tommy would be able to fit between the bars. Just in case he was there, we kept running. They were yelling threats to us for going in their pipe, but they didn't know who we were. I knew that because Gilly kept yelling, "I know who you are! I know who you are!" If he really knew, he would have called our names. He was bluffing.

Once we got on top again, we slowed down and started to walk back to Mr. Phillips'. If Little Tommy was on our tail, we could play it cool like we'd been there the whole time. In case we bumped into those guys later, we didn't want to look hot or anything. We were about a block away when I noticed that our feet and pants legs were wet. That would give us away for sure. We decided to head back home instead. We were both a little nervous still but were laughing because we'd gotten away.

Behind Phillips' store, Taylor handed me the gun. I dried it by dabbing at it, careful not to wipe off any prints. I was thinking how I would find a good hiding place for it when we saw all the cops and the television cameras. At first, I was excited to see all that action going on in our neighborhood, but Taylor stopped dead in his tracks. I was motioning him with my arm to run and see what all of it was about, but he was shaking his head.

Running the way we were—for our lives—made me think of that Latino kid again. I kind of knew how he must have felt. Only it was worse for him. He didn't know what he'd done. At least I knew what my crime was. I had broken the code. But that kid—he never knew.

It was weird that I was thinking of him right about the time the police found his body. It was weird that it all happened that way.

"They found him," Taylor said quietly, so quietly I couldn't hear him. But I saw his lips and knew what he had said. They had found the kid. We watched as two men carried up a stretcher. I swallowed hard, then looked at Taylor. There was an ambulance and everything. I blinked at Taylor. He was thinking the same thing I was—this was because of us.

We both just stood there in our own world when the police officer came up and started talking to us. He told us his name and started asking us questions about the kid. He asked if we had seen him around and had we seen any suspicious activity going on in the past few days, stuff like that. I can't really remember exactly what we were saying, but I remember what my heart felt like when I looked up and saw that Gilly and the others were standing behind us. I thought Taylor was going to pass out. I put my hand tight against my shirt where I was holding the gun and froze like a statue.

I told the cop that we had been in my house and never heard anything. Then I pulled Taylor's arm and walked away. As we walked off, I could hear the cop asking the Jags the same questions. He was telling them that the kid was badly beaten and asking if they had any idea who was responsible. I looked over my shoulder and caught Gilly's eye. He nodded slightly at me and then went back to giving the cop a hard time. He was trying to look cool, but I could tell he was terrified. He was probably afraid the kid would come to and finger them. They were such cowards, and Gilly was the worst of them. He was brave when he was in a gang, but alone, he was a wimp. He was saying things like, "If you guys were down here more often, this kind of thing wouldn't happen" and "Where were you when this happened?"

The other guys were nodding their heads, trying to act cool, but they were just as scared as Gilly.

THIRTEEN

THE meeting was to take place at exactly 8:00 at St. Ives Baptist Church. By 7:45, the place was so packed with community leaders, people from all different neighborhoods, and news crews that it was hard to find a place to sit. It was already hot inside the building, and everyone was fanning. Ma, Reverend Loe, another pastor, and some political-looking guys were at the front of the church talking to a reporter holding a microphone. There was a gentle buzzing around the rest of the church while people visited with one another, waiting for the great event to get under way.

I was in the back against the wall, checking out everyone as they came in. I knew Ripper was still laid up, but I had this funny feeling. I really didn't want to be there, but I couldn't really miss it. So I tried to lie low and watch who showed up. I got this burning feeling and looked across the room. My eyes locked with Little Tommy on the other side of the church. He was there with his mama. What a good little boy. Who would suspect that Little Tommy Watson was part of the Jags, probably packing right there in the church? We stared at each other. I hated his guts.

He was there to spy, and I knew if anything happened to my mama, I would hold Little Tommy personally responsible. Maybe this time he sensed it from me. Maybe he realized that if there was going to be a fair fight, a one-on-one, he didn't want any part of me. Clapping at the front of the church caused me to break off my gaze.

Ma was clapping her hands to get the crowd's attention. First, she thanked everyone for such a great turnout. Within minutes, she led into what had just happened on T Street between the Jags and T-Posse and how things were getting out of control, had been for some time, but that it wasn't too late to take back the streets. There was a loud applause. Some people stood up and said their piece, told some kind of story about how they were mugged, beaten, scared off. Ripper's name came up again and again. T. J.'s name was mentioned a couple of times too.

Then Ma started up again. Her voice thundered through the church. She talked about her boy, how she loved her boy, and how she was doing this for her boy. People were nodding, fanning themselves, and agreeing loudly. Ma talked as she had done in my room, about how we had to decide what we wanted. *We* had to decide what was important to us. *We* had to have the courage to stand up for what we believed in.

She talked about how her boy was learning about Martin Luther King and Malcolm X. She talked about how they had had the courage to stand up for the people they loved, for the things they believed in.

"Thank you, Sister Williams," Reverend Loe stepped in, and there was more applause. Ma was a powerful speaker. Her voice had echoed off the walls, and her words were encouraged by people who were tired of Ripper and his ways. "I want to thank you for bringing up Dr. King because I think that is why we are all here. Like Dr. King, we have a dream too. Don't we? I say, don't we?" His voice boomed across the church, and there was loud acknowledgement, approval of his words. "We want peace for our children, for ourselves. We want to have a home where we are safe, where we can raise our families and teach our children to aspire to be good men and women!"

I looked back at Little Tommy. He was watching me. He wasn't hearing a word. He was so brainwashed by Ripper and the Jags, he couldn't even listen anymore. He was like some sick little robot. It didn't matter what Ma or the Reverend said; it wasn't going to stop. That was written all over Little Tommy's face. It wasn't going to stop without a fight.

Little Tommy turned back to Ma. He did that on purpose. He did it to let me see that he was there and he *knew* what Ma had said about Ripper.

For the next hour the police, the pastor, and the neighbors all talked about the problems and what we could do about them. But I didn't hear anything that would make Ripper go away. Reverend Loe and Ma were elected to head up a permanent committee to fight the crime and the gangs. At last, everyone broke for refreshments that had been supplied by the church and Mrs. Clements. Everyone applauded Mrs. Clements for the fine way she set up the table of juice and cookies, and they headed for snacks. Little Tommy sauntered over toward me and leaned against the wall real cool-like, placing one foot up on the wall behind him.

"Your mama's a good speaker," he said.

"Uh huh."

"Why she got it so bad for Ripper?"

"Why'd you beat up Taylor?" I asked after a minute or two of silence.

"That couldn't be helped, man," he shrugged. Poor Little Tommy, forced to beat up Taylor, three against one.

"It couldn't be helped," I repeated, not sure how to say anything back to that stupid remark.

"Man, why you wanna go and mess this up? You got a good deal goin'." He looked over at me, like he was trying to get on my good side. "Ripper liked you, man. You had real potential." He stressed the word po-ten-tial just like Ripper would have, and I cringed. They were all mindless robots.

"I never had a good thing goin'," I said, not looking at him. I watched as people picked through the cookies.

"You coulda made some good money. Helped out your mama, you know?"

"Your mama know what you do?" I suddenly asked. He shrugged and looked over toward her. She was up front talking to the pastor. It was almost funny. If she only knew.

"She don't care. She knows I got a good after-school job that helps out with rent, you know?"

"Uh huh."

We were quiet for a couple of minutes. I was thinking about what Ma had asked me. I did have goals. I guess I never realized it until I had said it out loud, but I wanted more than all this. I wanted the same things Ma wanted.

"What are your goals?" I asked Little Tommy, and he looked at me like I was insane. "In life, man, what do you want?"

"Oh, I'm gonna get it," he laughed. "Cars, women, big house." He rattled it off, laughing at the thought. "Money," he added after some thought, "lots of money."

"How you gonna get all that?" I looked at him.

"See, that's what I'm trying to tell you, man. You stick with Ripper, and these things are gonna happen. Like I'm standing here, it could all be yours!"

❖ ❖ ❖

It was one of the hardest things I'd ever considered—turning on my homeboys. You know, it breaks this code of the streets. You just don't do it. But it was a choice between them and my mama, my family. It was between them and Taylor. There wasn't a choice anymore.

Taylor was really caught. He still loved his brother no matter what, and he wanted Brad to think he was cool, but he could never forgive

Ripper for what he had done. Plus, he knew what a real creep Ripper was. He knew Brad was a punk too, but it was hard to admit, so he just pretended that he didn't care. He was stuck. He couldn't rat out his own brother. And if he did, Brad might be the one to kill him. Brad was a loser.

Taylor still acted funny around me. It was really hard, and I felt sorry for him. Taylor was the kind of guy who needed a leader, someone he could follow. When we were tight, it wasn't so much that I was the leader, but he could fall back on me. He knew that no matter what, he had me by his side, but now it was like he was confused. He didn't have his brother anymore, and he didn't have me. I knew what a punk Brad was.

I saw Taylor at school and on the bus, and that was about it. The swelling in his face went down, and he was looking like his old self again.

That whole time seems like one of Grandma's stories—we were all frozen with our mouths open waiting for the commercial. All of us were frozen, and no one was doing anything. The Jones sisters, Taylor, me—none of us doing anything to help. So I kept writing in my journal about the kid. I'd get mad about that stupid kid, and I would write. The journal was due on

Friday. I had two days to finish something else or turn that one in and break the code—I mean, *really* break the code. I wrote in the journal for the last time.

❈ ❈ ❈

This is the neighborhood where the ice cream man can't come and you hardly ever see the police. You can't get scared 'cause it'll tear you up, so you have to get mad. Some people get beat up when they come into the neighborhood because they don't belong, and others get beat up just because they're there. People have to start making a stand, like breaking the code of the streets.

This is my neighborhood, and I don't like it. I want it to stop. I want Ripper to go away, and I want the carjackings to stop. I want kids to be able to see their mothers, and I want crime to stop. I want all murder to stop. I want to live in a neighborhood where everyone likes everyone, and no one is afraid to go outside. I want to go to a school that is in my neighborhood, and there are lots of books for all the kids, and everyone can learn. I want to live somewhere else, but I can't. I think if I was a leader, I would make it stop. I would find a way to make it better so people could stop being mad and afraid, so they could work together, not fight one another, so no one would have to follow guys like Ripper. If I was a leader, I would work to get rid of gangs and to help the people who want a better life and care about other people. A real leader would break the code of silence and not be afraid!

My grandma told me that when the time came, she knew that I would make the right decision. Alberto Salvazar didn't know any better, but I guess I do.

❈ ❈ ❈

I got an A, if that means anything. I guess it does since it's all part of my goal. I showed it to Ms. Whitley so she'd know I did it, then I turned it over to Officer Kelly. He had been there at the "Taking Back Our Streets" meeting.

I named the Jones sisters and Taylor as witnesses to the Salvazar beating, but Ma dropped off the gun in a paper bag with a note to check prints. That one we left as an anonymous tip, just to be safe. Ma was real proud of me: I got the A; and Ripper, Gilly, and Brad would be spending most of their time in juvenile detention or jail. Little Tommy was in trouble; how much, I really didn't know.

We thought it was over until we got a knock on the door. I was in my room when I heard Ma call me out. There was a reporter and a photographer from the *Washington Post* with the police chief. They gave me the $10,000 Salvazar reward. Ma's mouth just fell open.

"What?"

"Yes, ma'am," the reporter said, and the photographer fell back to take a picture. Ma grabbed me up in her arms and hugged me.

"Ten thousand dollars," she practically yelled. She couldn't believe it. I couldn't believe it. The reporter kept asking me questions, but I didn't know what to say; I was in shock. All I could think about was how Ma could quit her night job. She could quit her night job!

"Oh, honey," Grandma said, hugging me. "I'm so proud of you. You see, you did the right thing. Now look, your mama can quit her night job."

"Oh," Ma whirled around and hugged me again. She hugged the reporter. "Oh, yes! Oh, Lord, yes! I can quit that awful job!"

The photographer took tons of pictures, and Ma and Grandma talked on and on until the reporter finally said he had what he needed and backed down the stairs. Ma and Grandma were just so excited, they were talking a mile a minute, and I was sure they never once heard what the other was saying.

They each fell into a kitchen chair and began talking at the same time about what we could do with the money, and, oh, we'd better be careful how we spend it, and Ma reached over and hugged me again. She was crying, she was so happy.

Pop!

At once all three of us looked at the stove, and Grandma laughed.

"Well, I know one member of the family that won't be here too much longer!"

"Oh, yes!" Ma was clapping her hands. "Yes, yes, yes!" She whirled around in her seat and faced off with the stove. "Your days are numbered, Mr. Stove!"

"Oh, Lord, this is indeed a good day!" Grandma leaned over and gave my hand a squeeze. I smiled and sat back in my chair, watching Ma threaten the stove.

Pop!

It was kind of funny except I couldn't help thinking about that stupid kid. Ma could quit her night job, and maybe we could move. And a new stove. A new stove 'cause I watched a kid get killed.

"What's the matter, baby?" Ma suddenly stopped her dance and looked at me.

"Huh?" I tried to smile, but it didn't really work. "Nothing. I was just thinking."

"What? What is it?" she pressed. I told her, and she sat down.

It just didn't seem right, you know? I couldn't get that kid out of my head. It was stupid. It's not like I could undo what had happened. I put my head down on the table.

Pop!

We all looked at the stove. No one said anything for a long time.

"It's really not that bad of a stove," Ma said finally.

I lifted my head and looked at Ma. She sighed, looked back at me, and smiled.

FOURTEEN

THE empty lot next to the new market on corner of T Street and 15th became the new home of the Alberto Salvazar Recreational Center. It became a place where kids can go after school to play basketball, table tennis, games, whatever, just to stay off the streets. Student interns from Howard University come to tutor kids in all different subjects. They call it "giving back to the community."

It is painted bright red and yellow on the bricks outside. A huge rainbow is painted over the front steps to the building. On one side of the rainbow there is a mural of Martin Luther King, and on the other is Malcolm X. The picture looks like they are leading children behind them so that they will come together. It's really cool-looking—the kind of picture that makes you stop and think about things. And the more I look at their faces, the more I like them.

There are new balls, equipment, and books. Everything, all the funding, was donated by the private sector, and the Alberto Salvazar Recreational Center is run by a beautiful woman named Ms. Carmen Williams, but everyone calls her Ma.

Pop!